Leslie Charteris'

Count on the Saint

By Leslie Charteris

DARE DEVIL
THE BANDIT
THE WHITE RIDER
X ESQUIRE

The Saint Series in order of sequence

MEET THE TIGER!
ENTER THE SAINT
THE SAINT CLOSES THE CASE
THE AVENGING SAINT
FEATURING THE SAINT
ALIAS THE SAINT
THE SAINT MEETS HIS MATCH
THE SAINT V. SCOTLAND YARD
THE SAINT'S GETAWAY
THE SAINT AND MR. TEAL
THE BRIGHTER BUCCANEER
THE SAINT IN LONDON
THE SAINT INTERVENES
THE SAINT GOES ON
THE SAINT IN NEW YORK
THE SAINT OVERBOARD
ACE OF KNAVES
THE SAINT BIDS DIAMONDS
THE SAINT PLAYS WITH FIRE
FOLLOW THE SAINT
THE HAPPY HIGHWAYMAN
THE SAINT IN MIAMI
THE SAINT GOES WEST
THE SAINT STEPS IN
THE SAINT ON GUARD
THE SAINT SEES IT THROUGH
CALL FOR THE SAINT
SAINT ERRANT
THE SAINT IN EUROPE
THE SAINT ON THE SPANISH MAIN
THANKS TO THE SAINT
THE SAINT AROUND THE WORLD
SEÑOR SAINT
THE SAINT TO THE RESCUE
TRUST THE SAINT
THE SAINT IN THE SUN
VENDETTA FOR THE SAINT
THE SAINT ON T.V.
THE SAINT RETURNS
THE SAINT AND THE FICTION MAKERS
THE SAINT ABROAD
THE SAINT'S CHOICE
THE SAINT IN PURSUIT
THE SAINT AND THE PEOPLE IMPORTERS
CATCH THE SAINT
THE SAINT AND THE HAPSBURG NECKLACE
SEND FOR THE SAINT
THE SAINT IN TROUBLE
THE SAINT AND THE TEMPLAR TREASURE
COUNT ON THE SAINT

Leslie Charteris'

Count on the Saint:

The Pastor's Problem & The Unsaintly Santa

Original Outlines by Donne Avenell

Developed by
GRAHAM WEAVER

PUBLISHED FOR THE CRIME CLUB BY
DOUBLEDAY & COMPANY, INC.
GARDEN CITY, NEW YORK
1980

All of the characters in this book are fictitious, and any resemblance to actual persons, living or dead, is purely coincidental.

ISBN: 0-385-17191-9
Library of Congress Catalog Card Number: 80-939

Printed in the United States of America
First Edition

Contents

Leslie Charteris'

Count on the Saint

I

The Pastor's Problem

1

The peace-loving, law-abiding residents of Upper Berkeley Mews had long ago become inured to the presence of their celebrated neighbour, though whether his decision to be domiciled amongst them was to be welcomed they had never quite decided. True, he added a certain glamour to that otherwise staid and soporific backwater, but on the other hand there was the ever present threat that he might one day bring his work home with him, so causing the tranquillity to be disturbed by undignified skylarking. Being British, and from that stratum of society which considers it bad form to discuss anything more private than the weather with anyone who has not been formally introduced, they compromised. They affected to ignore him, hoping he would reciprocate. At the same time they avidly read of his activities and kept a weather eye on his comings and goings to provide them with a ceaseless supply of gossip guaranteed to keep the conversation flowing over cocktails or coffee.

Their attitude was understandable. When the man next door is a criminal, a certain sense of insecurity is predictable; when he is the most notorious and successful outlaw of his age, it is inevitable.

For his part, Simon Templar was aware of their feelings and welcomed their reserve, for they saw only what he wanted them to see, and their reluctance to bother him in even the little of his private life that they did witness enabled him to go about his business unhampered by trivial interferences.

Any of his neighbours who saw him return home at ten o'clock one blustery September night in 1950 would have found nothing strange about either his actions or his appearance as he slotted his key into the lock.

They would have observed a tall athletic man with the permanently light tan of the seasoned traveller. If there was a certain piratical cast to the features and a subtly dangerous quality to the way he moved, these were only to be expected. They would have noticed that he was wearing a dark blue suit that hung with the millimetric precision that only the very best tailors achieve, with a silk shirt of such virginal whiteness that it might have been newly bought that morning. But being accustomed to seeing him so dressed, they would simply have concluded that he had enjoyed an early dinner, probably at one of the better hostelries, where he had doubtless selected the best food and the finest wines with the ease of the accomplished gourmet. And they would have been right.

Any of them still keeping an eye on his home ten minutes later would have seen the front door open and watched him emerge once again into the mews. They would have noted that he now wore a dark leather casual jacket, dark grey trousers, and a navy-blue rollneck sweater, and that the thin leather shoes had been replaced by a pair of workmanlike brogues. The rapid transformation might have caused an eyebrow to be raised and created a suspicion that he was up to no good. But he carried, of all inoffensive burdens, a plain black and somewhat shabby violin case. It suggested at once a minor musician on his way to work at some night club.

Simon Templar did not know whether he was under surveillance and he did not care. He walked briskly out of the mews and through the quiet Mayfair side streets until he reached Piccadilly, where he turned left. He considered hailing a taxi but decided against the idea. The traffic was crawling along even on that broad thoroughfare, and as his destination lay beyond a maze of narrow streets which at that time of night would be clotted with parked cars he realised it would be almost as quick to walk.

A few hundred yards later he arrived in Piccadilly Circus.

The Circus is the hub of London and the centre of what the guidebook writers are wont to call the "Bright Lights," though any New Yorker would be surprised at the economy of syncopated neon employed to justify the description. To the tourist it is a sight to see, one more landmark ticked off the holiday itinerary. To the Londoner it is a symbol, even if he would find it hard to explain exactly what it symbolises. The attraction of the handful of major roads and minor side streets which tie themselves into a knot around the foot of the statue of Eros is not something that can be seen; it has to be felt.

Whenever there is an excuse for national celebration it is to Piccadilly Circus that the crowds flock, as if drawn by some giant invisible magnet. It is on the pavements of Piccadilly that the starry-eyed provincial in search of adventure and fame in the big city is most likely to first put down his—or more usually her—suitcase. Soldiers have sung their goodbyes to it, and Eros has become as national a symbol as the Eiffel Tower, the Statue of Liberty, or the onion domes of the Kremlin.

Perhaps part of its appeal is that it brings together four of the most famous districts of the capital: the shops of Regent Street with the theatres of Shaftesbury Avenue; Mayfair, which has become a byword for all that is English, elegant, and aristocratic; and Soho, which has become synonymous with the cosmopolitan, the tawdry, and the criminal.

Simon Templar turned to skirt the central island of the Circus and flicked up his jacket collar in token resistance to the drizzle that had just started to drain from an overcast sky. Anyone seeing him there might have thought it an appropriate place. Half an hour before, he had been relaxing in the sophisticated surroundings of a Mayfair restaurant. In another thirty minutes he would be equally at home attending to his business in the shabby streets of Soho.

It is part of the folklore of London that if you stand in Piccadilly Circus long enough you will eventually meet everyone you ever knew. At ten-forty that night the claim was almost believable. Cinemas and theatres disgorged their audiences onto the streets, and some were hurrying in search of supper while the early evening revellers were leaving the pubs and clubs in search of home. Swelling the jostling crowds were end-of-season tourists and that miscellaneous collection of unpigeonholeable characters who are to be found loitering at any time of the day, and most hours of the night, in every great meeting place in every great city of the world. The flotsam and jetsam of society, constantly changing faces that always look the same.

The public read about the Saint's exploits and marvelled at his audacity. To them it must have appeared that he suddenly materialised in the right place at the right time as if by divine guidance. The usual fact, however, was that the events they digested with their bacon and eggs were the culmination of careful preparation, a major factor of which is attention to the minutiae of the task in hand. It was therefore no whim that had decided the time for his foray. For the next half hour the area would be at its busiest and he understood the value of the anonymity of crowds.

He dodged nimbly between the fenders of the cars inching into and out of Regent Street, crossed Glasshouse Street, and cut across the corner of the Regent Palace Hotel to turn up Sherwood Street. Within a dozen paces the lights and some of the exhaust fumes were left behind, and the shadows swallowed him. He turned right on Brewer Street; it was not the shortest way to his destination, but it was less congested, and he was able to maintain a brisker pace until he reached the junction with Wardour Street.

One of the delights of London is that the sprawling metropolis shown on the map is in reality just a collection of villages that the highways of the capital have threaded together without destroying their separate identities. Nowhere can this be more plainly seen than in the square mile lying between Oxford Street, Regent Street, Shaftesbury Avenue, and Charing Cross Road. In some ways Soho is not only a village within a city, it is almost a state within a country, and its boundaries are as tangible to those who live and work within them as the more conventional frontiers of mountains and rivers. Its people are drawn from every corner of Europe, many of them refugees from tyranny or poverty who have settled there and made it their own.

Soho is a place of restaurants where in one street the aromas of paella, bouillabaisse, goulash, and lasagne ride the air along with the music of half a dozen different tongues. Most of all it is a place of people who provide proof that different creeds and complexions can exist peacefully side by side.

But there is also a darker, more dangerous undercurrent. Before the first immigrants arrived, Soho was already established as the red light district of London. The houses of pleasure which Victorian gentlemen patronised had long since disappeared and been replaced by streetwalkers and their more discreet sisters who plied their trade via carefully worded advertisements in news agents' windows. The vice trade has spawned every type of crime and breed of criminal, from those selling pictures that would make a Port Said pedlar blush to those who deal in the death that comes from a syringe. Violence and danger lie very close to the surface and invest Soho with an excitement that is found nowhere else in London.

East of Wardour Street, the Saint zigzagged through smaller lanes in the direction of Soho Square, and as he did so drew a pair of thin black leather gloves from his pocket and pulled them on. On another side street, he stopped and appeared to consider the menu displayed in the window of an Italian restaurant that stood on the corner of a cobbled alley. And then he was gone.

The shadows cast by the walls of the buildings each

side of the narrow entrance enveloped him immediately. The operation was carried out so slickly that anyone only a few steps behind would have missed it in the time it took them to blink. Had any of his neighbours who earlier might have wondered at his change of clothes been following, the reason for the switch now became obvious. It is very rarely completely dark in a city in the way it often is in the country. Even if the night is starless the light from windows and the glow of street lamps keeps the blackness at bay and replaces it with an ever shifting variety of deep blues and purples and a hundred shades of grey. In such a situation a man dressed in black can stand out almost as distinctly as one in white, but the combination of subdued colours the Saint had chosen blended perfectly with his surroundings.

The alley led into a small courtyard where the squares of light from the windows of the buildings that formed its perimeter laid an irregular checkerboard of yellow and black across the flagstones. Simon kept close to the walls and moved slowly and cautiously until he reached the building immediately opposite the entrance.

He stopped there to take from his pocket a length of string already knotted to form a circle. Looped through the handle of the violin case, over his head and under one arm, it became a sling which suspended the case behind his shoulders and left his hands free.

He was at the rear of a four-storey house, and beside it, so close that a man could not have walked between them, was a square tower topped by a spire and what remained of one wall of the church it had once dominated. A donation from the Luftwaffe had put a permanent end to its services. The roof was gone, and the windows in the tower and wall had been boarded up. Two giant props rose from the interior to support the tower, one side of which seemed to consist more of boards and tarpaulin sheets than of stone.

Simon placed both hands around the drainpipe on the tower end of the house, braced his feet against the brickwork, and began to climb. As he scaled the wall he paid a silent tribute to the Victorian builder's love of exterior plumbing and wide window ledges that enabled him, despite the slipperiness of the wet metal and smooth stone, to reach his goal as quickly and easily as if he had brought a ladder.

The only difficulty arose when he reached the top-floor window and had to hold onto the pipe with one hand while he took a roll of sticky tape from his pocket and crisscrossed it on the glass. That operation completed, he leaned outward and brought the flat of his forearm against the pane. It shuddered and cracked with the first blow, and the second shattered it and sent it into the room without the noise of cascading glass.

He swung himself onto the window ledge, grabbed the top half of the sash window, and used it as a support as he slid into the room. Only after he had drawn the heavy curtains and paused to listen for any indication that his entrance had been heard did he take a small flashlight from his pocket. Silver foil had been stuck over the glass so that just a needle-thin stream of light escaped but it was enough to show him the general layout of the room and pinpoint the safe in the corner.

He crossed and knelt before the safe, unhitching the violin case and putting it down. From inside his jacket he took a soft leather roll, untied it, and spread it out on the floor beside him. The Saint was very proud of that roll: it contained a collection of precision instruments, many made to his own design, that would have earned instant promotion for any policeman fortunate enough to find them on him. He inspected the lock of the safe and then extracted the tool required. With the torch between his teeth so that its light was focused steadily on the lock, he went to work.

The lock was complex and included a triple lever mechanism that made it a problem even for someone of his experience. He concentrated intently on the delicate probing and turning of the instrument gripped tightly between his thumb and forefinger, his ears straining to pick up the whisper of a click that would tell him the first stage was over. When it came he allowed himself the luxury of a brief pause while he took a deep steadying breath. He returned to work but had barely begun when a noise on the landing outside made him stop.

It was followed by the sound every burglar dreads. The handle rattled, a key grated in the lock, and the door behind him started to open.

2

He spun around, every nerve and sinew taut, ready to attack or defend on the instant.

The door swung fully open to reveal a lone figure on the threshold. Simon stayed motionless and waited. The man stepped into the study and raised his hand to the light switch.

Simon blinked at the sudden brilliance as the man walked casually to within a few feet and stood looking down at him. Delving deep into the pocket of his robe, the man produced a key and held it out to him.

"Puedo ayudarte?"

Simon sat back on his haunches and waited for the adrenalin to dissolve and his muscles to relax before replying.

When he did speak, it was in an urgent whisper:

"Father Bernardo, for heaven's sake! I'm supposed to be robbing you!"

The priest smiled.

"For heaven's sake? No. For pity's sake? Yes," he said in a gentle voice which bore only the faintest trace of an accent.

The Saint sighed in exasperation as he stood up.

"For whosever sake it is, especially for my sake, let me get on with the burglary."

"I am sorry, I did not think you would come so soon."

"Next time I'll hang a notice outside and you can charge admission. If you're going to stay, don't interrupt."

"*Dispénsame*, I will not bother you again," the priest promised, in such a contrite tone that the Saint could not help smiling.

He had robbed many people in the course of his criminal career, but never had he dealt with such a helpful and willing victim. He switched off the now superfluous torch and returned his attention to the intricacies of the lock. The priest sat quietly and calmly on the far side of the room and watched.

Father Bernardo looked older and frailer than his sixty years. The voluminous folds of his cassock highlighted his thinness, and his sparse white hair added to the overall effect of making him seem smaller and weaker than he was. Despite the gauntness of a face that had once been more than passably handsome, the eyes still sparkled with kindness and good humour, and there were the lines of many smiles at the corners of his mouth. But Simon knew that the image of a genial, fragile old man was deceptive and that the priest possessed reserves of strength and stamina that a man twenty years his junior might have envied.

They had first met during the tail-end days of the Spanish Civil War when Franco's soldiers and agents were rounding up all those who had opposed him. Father Bernardo had been the pastor of a small town in Aragon and from the start had defied the official line of his church and preached in favour of the Republicans. By the time the Falangists marched into the region to mop up the last of the resistance he was already a marked man.

As the Fascists drew nearer, the townspeople begged him to flee but he refused. Only when they implored him to take the children and the treasures of their church to the safety of a nearby monastery did he relent. By the time his mission was completed the town had been occupied and there was no going back. And so he had set out on the long journey into exile.

It was on that road that he had met the Saint and in the few days they had spent together a mutual respect and liking had flowered. Simon Templar's activities in the madness that was to prove merely a dress rehearsal for a much greater insanity have yet to be chronicled; but for now it must be enough to say that they had shared more than one adventure before Father Bernardo eventually crossed the Pyrenees. But the megalomania of Franco's principal sponsor had made his stay in France a comparatively short one, and he became a refugee for the second time. In the blitzed wreckage of St. Jude's he at last found another home.

His first action was to open the crypt as a sanctuary for fellow outcasts. At first they had come from many lands submerged in the world turmoil, but by now most of them had been gradually replaced by the destitute and the rejected of his adopted country.

He refused no one help or shelter, but quickly found that those who were the first to applaud his charity were usually the last to dig into their pockets for the cash to make it possible. One by one the church valuables he had brought with him were sold in order to keep St. Jude's open. Now only one remained. Which was why Simon Templar was picking the safe lock and Father Bernardo was watching him.

Simon had renewed their acquaintance as soon as he heard that Bernardo had arrived in London, but the nature of his vocation and his constant travelling had resulted in long gaps between meetings. A call at the church the previous day had been the first for nearly a year. His reception had been as warm as always, but it was not long before he had detected the strain beneath the priest's smile.

The Saint gave a final twist to an instrument resembling an old-fashioned buttonhook and with a triumphant smile turned the handle and opened the door of the safe. Inside, on the single shelf, wrapped in a black velvet cloth, rested the object he sought. He took it out and placed it on the desk before removing the cloth.

It was an intricately engraved silver chalice about ten inches high. Carved in relief around the cup were the Stations of the Cross, while on the cover was depicted the Last Supper. Around the base were set evenly spaced rows of semi-precious stones, and the handles were formed by ornately sculptured golden crucifixes.

"It's very beautiful," Simon observed softly.

Father Bernardo sighed.

"Yes, it is beautiful. But beauty will not buy bread or pay for clothes or purchase coal. My people are not concerned with beauty but with survival."

They had reverted to Spanish, which to the Saint had once been almost another native language.

The old priest's words were an echo of the conversation that had passed between them the day before and which had led to that night's activity. Father Bernardo had needed little prompting to tell the Saint his troubles. St. Jude's had always existed on the borderline between solvency and bankruptcy, but rising costs and a fall in donations had finally combined to push the sanctuary over the edge. Simon's first reaction to the news had been to reach for his cheque book, but before he could make his offer Father Bernardo had shown him the chalice. He had been unusually bitter.

"Look at it," he had invited his guest with an impatient, almost angry sweep of his arm. "It is worth a small fortune, a fraction of its value would save St. Jude's. It is useless to me, yet I cannot sell it."

In answer to the Saint's question he had explained that the chalice had been the most prized possession of his church, the richest and most valuable thing in the entire town. It had been given three hundred years ago in gratitude for some service, long since forgotten, that the villagers had rendered to a member of the royal family. But there had been a condition; it must never leave the custody of the priest.

"And so it stayed, beautiful but rarely used, while the

villagers lived in poverty. There was never any suggestion that it should be sold, such a thing was unthinkable and still is forbidden," the priest had complained, and his voice had trembled with suppressed frustration.

"What you might almost call treasure in heaven," said the Saint.

"It is a very common story. Far too common. Go into any cathedral in almost any Latin country and you will marvel at how magnificent it is, the sculptures and the carvings and the paintings and all the other priceless things. And then go outside and walk a little way and you will marvel again, but this time at the slums and the squalor, at the tenements and the children in ragged clothes and the despair on the faces of those whom poverty has made old before their time. The Church cares for its treasures and it cares if it can for the needy, but rarely is the one used for the other. That is not the way it should be, not the way it was meant to be. The true treasures of the Church are the poor, but the Church holds onto what it has and the poor can only dream of what they have not."

"And yet you wouldn't sell the chalice to save St. Jude's?" Simon had asked, wondering that Father Bernardo would be bound by something which was against his deep convictions.

The priest shook his head sadly.

"I could not, Simon. My people entrusted the chalice and the other church valuables to me when we knew that the Falangists were coming. I feel I have already betrayed them by selling the other things, even for the best of purposes, but they were not actually consecrated. The chalice is in my care under the most sacred vows, until I can take it back."

The Saint had considered the situation for a while and his immediate solution to the problem was one that the good pastor would not have thought of.

"Supposing," the Saint had asked conversationally, "supposing it was stolen. Would you keep the insurance money or send it to the people of your town?"

"It is not likely to happen."

"But if it did," Simon had persisted.

"Then I expect I would keep the money and use it to maintain St. Jude's. I should consider it a loan in a good cause, which my people might well approve. And I would pray that one day it might be repaid. But it will never happen."

Simon had smiled as he watched Father Bernardo rewrap the chalice and put it back in the safe.

"One certain thing in life is that you never know what is going to happen next," he said.

"I can be sure that what you have suggested will never happen," said the priest. "You see, the chalice is not insured. I could never afford the premiums."

For a moment the Saint had been stumped. But only for a moment.

"What then would you do if it was stolen and the thief had a sudden change of heart and sent you the money he got for it?" he asked.

The priest was silent for a long while as he considered the question.

"If such a road to Damascus occurred in the life of a criminal, I should be pleased and I would pray that he might be forgiven for his crime," was the eventual reply.

"And you would use the money to save St. Jude's?"

"Yes. But what is the good of thinking about such things? It would be a miracle."

Simon had put a reassuring arm around his shoulders. "I believe in miracles," he confided.

And then he had taken his leave and returned home to plan the details of what he had decided to do. Now that it had been accomplished there still remained the problem of whether Father Bernardo would agree to it.

He replaced the cloth over the chalice so that it was no longer either a distraction or a temptation.

"You guessed I might do this, Bernardo?" he asked.

"It was not hard. I know you too well, Simon, and the kind of solutions you find. Did you think I could not read what was in your mind?"

"No," Simon admitted. "But I hoped that you might prefer not to. I can still put the chalice back if that is what you want."

"What I want is to save St. Jude's. What you do with the chalice must now be your decision."

"And if I decide to take it?"

"I cannot stop you."

"But what will you say to the police?"

"I shall tell them that it has been stolen."

"Nothing more?"

Father Bernardo looked round the room, as if seeking an answer, and when he looked at the Saint again the smile that pulled at the corners of his mouth indicated that he had found one.

"My church is a ruin and this room is the nearest place I have to a confessional. People tell me many things here that I would never repeat. I can treat you no differently."

The Saint laughed. He opened the violin case and put the chalice inside.

"Then I think it's time to take my leave."

He slung the case over his shoulder as he had carried it

before, crossed to the window, and swung himself onto the ledge.

The priest raised his hands and parted them in blessing.

"*Pax vobiscum*, my son."

"*Hasta luego*, Papa Bernardo," said the Saint, and disappeared into the darkness.

He shinned down the drainpipe as nimbly as any sailor down the rigging of a becalmed galleon. He stepped backwards onto the ground, and in that same instant he felt a kind of dull shock in the back of his head and everything went black.

3

Actually his awareness of the impact was retrospective, when he woke up. It had been as neat a demonstration of the sandbagger's art as Simon Templar had ever had the misfortune to experience. The cushioned blow had done its job without even breaking the skin, let alone the skull. Its legacy would be little more than a tender bump and a hangover-style headache. He had been despatched out of the world for perhaps thirty seconds. But it was enough.

The first sense to break clear of the fog numbing his brain was hearing: the sound of running feet growing rapidly fainter as the attacker fled. Sight returned reluctantly: the blurred outlines of the grill of the drain that he was slumped beside. He screwed his eyes tight closed and then blinked them wide open, repeating the process until his vision cleared. Gripping the drainpipe with both hands, he groggily hoisted himself upright.

Leaning with his back against the wall, he sucked the cool night air into his lungs and looked around. The court was deserted. His gaze travelled upwards to the few squares of light in the surrounding buildings but he saw no one. He had hardly expected to. Even if the attack had been witnessed, Soho is an area where the residents' discretion makes the three wise monkeys appear congenital gossips when it comes to seeing, hearing, or speaking of the evil they may come across. Neither was he surprised to find that the violin case had gone, as well as his wallet.

The Saint uttered certain expletives of Anglo-Saxon origin fluently and forcefully during the few seconds he spent casting about for some clue to his attacker, but the man had left no trace. If indeed it was a man, Simon told himself ruefully: for all he knew it could have been a dowager duchess in full ermine regalia.

The light was still burning in Father Bernardo's study above him, and for a moment he considered returning via the front door and explaining the situation. But what could he say? "I've been robbed" perhaps, or "You'll never guess what just happened to me." No, he decided, it would be better to leave him in happy ignorance while there was still a chance of getting the chalice back.

The thief had left enough small change in his trouser pocket for a taxi fare, but the Saint felt that a walk would help to clear his head and provide time to think.

He began to retrace the route he had taken an hour before. Then his mission had been as straightforward as any he had ever undertaken. Now, in less than a minute, everything had been turned upside down and confusion had replaced simplicity.

He turned right into Shaftesbury Avenue towards Piccadilly Circus. The throbbing at the base of his skull subsided as he walked and allowed his brain to grapple methodically with the problems he now faced.

There was no profit in damning the vagaries of fate, no point in looking back. He had to concentrate on questions that might be answered productively.

Had the sandbag artist been waiting for him? Unlikely. Not even Father Bernardo had known precisely when the Saint would come. Therefore, had the attack been spontaneous? Most possibly; although the court was little used and so not the most likely place for a footpad to lurk. But could the mugger have been planning a break-in on his own, and been happy to watch the Saint do it for him and hijack the proceeds? If so, was he after the chalice or just anything that might come his way? Square one again.

It might seem to be a detail of stupendous unimportance, whether he had been robbed of the chalice with intent or purely by bad luck. If it was by accident, as soon as the thief discovered what he had stolen, it would be quickly funnelled into one of the normal markets for stolen goods: if it was with intent, the problem could be infinitely more complicated.

The irony of the situation was not lost on the Saint. Despite his anger, he could acknowledge it with a rueful smile. The Robin Hood of Modern Crime, the newspapers had dubbed him, and he had more than lived up to the title, robbing the ungodly rich and giving the loot to the poor—minus a respectable percentage to cover his expenses. Much of his career had been spent thieving from thieves and now the tables had been turned. It might be poetic, Simon reflected as he arrived back at Upper Berkeley Mews, but on this particular occasion it was certainly not justice.

His only immediate solution, as it had been with many another riddle, was to sleep on it. But in this case the prescription failed to work. Sleep removed the physical pain but did nothing to soothe the hurt to his pride, nor did he awake with the inspiration he had hoped for. The problems of the dark were just as unanswerable in the light.

But if he thought they were difficult enough, he did not have to wait long to be shown their true proportionate triviality.

He had dealt with a late breakfast, showered, and dressed when the doorbell rang. He recognised his visitor with a smile of pleasure and appreciation, and held the door wide for her to enter.

"Buenos días, Mila!" he said.

Mila is short for *Milagrosa,* which in Spanish means miraculous, and so is an apt choice of name for the niece of a priest. The last time Simon had seen her she had been a skinny schoolgirl scarcely out of pigtails, but two years can see many changes at that age.

Now, although she could still have been barely old enough to vote, she had a refined beauty that Goya would have paid to paint. The sheen of the long black hair which swirled across her face when she turned her head, the pout of her lips, the mystery and promise of dark flashing eyes, and a figure that curved in exactly the right places and proportions were as much as any man, artist or not, could have asked for. Perhaps one day the smooth skin would wrinkle and the taut figure would spread, but that would not be for a long time to come.

Simon closed the door and turned.

"Well, well!" His eyes flicked unashamedly over the girl and widened with approval. "I won't say 'Haven't you grown'—just tell me what happened to the pimply little girl who used to put itching powder in the cassocks."

Mila smiled.

"I left her behind at the convent."

"Those poor sisters," he murmured. "Bernardo told me you were helping at the mission now. I'd hoped to see you but you were out running a soup kitchen or something."

"Collecting jumble, actually. He told me you'd called."

Her voice was strained. She stood awkwardly in the centre of the room, nervously fingering her handbag. Simon read the signs and nodded towards a chair.

"Sit down and tell me what's on your mind. You haven't dropped in just to chat."

Mila shook her head. She perched on the edge of the cushion while the Saint lowered himself at a more comfortable angle into the neighbouring chair. She did not speak at once and he allowed her time to collect her thoughts. He could guess that at least part of her reason for visiting him was a result of the previous night's skylarking, and her first words confirmed his prescience.

"We've been robbed. Last night someone broke in and stole a chalice . . ."

"The one the villagers gave to your uncle for safekeeping?" he enquired innocently.

"Yes, it's very valuable. Uncle is terribly upset about it."

"I can imagine."

The Saint suppressed a smile. He hoped the priest wasn't hamming it up too much.

"I shouldn't get too alarmed," he continued soothingly. "The police are really far cleverer than those writer blokes would have you believe. I'm sure they'll get it back, though I don't hold out much hope of them catching the man who took it."

"But that's just it," said Mila despairingly, her eyes shining with tears. "They already have."

4

It is a testimonial to Simon Templar's self-control that not even the faintest flicker of reaction crossed his face. His features maintained the same interested but detached expression. But behind the façade it was as if floodgates had opened to release a fresh torrent of questions and problems that threatened temporarily to submerge the ones he was already wrestling with.

"You mean," he asked in a voice empty of any emotion, "that the police caught the thief who stole the chalice?"

"Yes, I mean no, I mean . . ." Mila paused, took a breath, and began again. "What I really mean is that they've arrested who they think did it. But he didn't. He couldn't have done. They've got the wrong person."

Simon regarded her steadily.

"I have a feeling that this conversation is about to get complicated, so before we get entangled in it I think some lubrication is called for."

He crossed to the drinks cabinet, looked from the array of bottles to the girl, and raised an enquiring eyebrow.

"Coffee?"

She nodded.

"Thank you."

He handed her a cup.

"What makes you think the constabulary have fingered the wrong collar?" he asked.

"They've arrested Taffy, Taffy Owen. But he didn't do it. He couldn't have done," Mila replied, her voice rising in protest.

"So you've already said," Simon remarked calmly. "Let's get down to basics. First question: who is this Taffy Owen, besides being a son of the valleys?"

"He helps out at the mission. He's been there just over a year. He got into some trouble at home—Cardiff—and came to London. Uncle found him sleeping rough and brought him back to the mission for the night, and he's stayed ever since. He was a bit wild at first, it's true, but he's settled down now."

"So Taffy's a sheep returned to the fold," the Saint said, and hoped it didn't sound too cynical. "Question two: how do you know he didn't do it?"

The query was innocent enough on the surface but there was a dual reason behind it. He already knew the answer, but he needed to know whether Mila did as well. Had Bernardo told her? Her reply was open enough to convince him that her uncle had kept silent.

"It's just not in his nature," she explained. "Once, perhaps, but not now. He thinks far too much of Uncle Bernardo, and . . ." She paused and mumbled the final few words of the sentence: ". . . and of me."

Simon's eyebrows rose only enough to make his point. "And you of him?"

A blush highlighted her smooth olive cheeks. She continued to avoid his eyes.

"I like him, if that's what you mean," she answered at length.

The Saint's smile lingered thoughtfully.

"It wasn't all I meant, but we'll let it pass. So the police have Taffy. Do they also have the chalice?"

The Saint was aware of a slight quickening of his pulse as he waited for her reply, and wasn't sure whether he was disappointed or relieved when he was told that the chalice had not yet been found.

"I came to you because Uncle Bernardo said you would know what to do," Mila went on. "He has great trust in you. He said that if anyone could prove Taffy's innocence you could."

"You don't say? I'm touched by his faith in me," Simon said drily. "Then I mustn't let him down. Where did they take Taffy?"

"To Vine Street police station."

"And do you know who's in charge of the case?"

"An Inspector Peake."

"Then I'd better go and make him see the error of his ways," he said with a lightness he was far from feeling. "Tell your uncle I will do everything I can."

He walked her to Bruton Street and kept the conversation superficial until he could put her in a cab despatched towards St. Jude's, while he began the short stroll to Vine Street.

"This is the last time I do anyone a favour by robbing them," he vowed to himself as he contemplated the latest twist of events.

In a shade over twelve hours what had started out as a simple well-intentioned felony had turned into an imbroglio of bedlamic dimensions. Besides having lost the chalice and facing the job of retrieving it, he was now presented with the problem of absolving a third party from having stolen it, without incriminating either himself or Father Bernardo. He could imagine the old priest's quite unholy glee as he blandly suggested to his niece that she should ask the Saint to help. It was easily the most magnificently brazen piece of buck-passing that could ever have been performed.

Simon wished, not for the first time, that he had opted for the easy solution and just written a cheque he could easily afford and so saved St. Jude's Mission and himself a lot of trouble.

But was this Taffy character as innocent as Mila and her uncle believed? Certainly he hadn't taken the chalice from the safe, but it had been stolen twice and someone had to be guilty of the second theft, so why not he?

At Vine Street police station the desk sergeant told him:

"Inspector Peake is at lunch. Can anyone else help you?"

Simon shook his head.

"No, I could do with a drink myself."

As expected, he found the man he wanted, together with some other non-uniformed members of C Division resting his elbows on the counter of the nearest hostelry. He had no difficulty recognising the detective. He regarded it as part of his professionalism to know by sight most of the West End's officers above the rank of sergeant, but to date Peake had not crossed his path.

The Saint edged into an empty slot at the bar beside the detective and ordered a pint of Guinness. As it was being pulled he turned to his neighbour.

"Inspector Peake. I'd like a word."

The detective ran a practised eye over the man who had interrupted his meditative midday drink. He took in the supple strength, the poise and the tanned features, and felt he should have known the name before he asked for it.

"And who are you?"

"Templar, Simon Templar. I'm interested in Taffy Owen. Can we talk?"

"The Saint?" Peake didn't try to keep the surprise out of his voice or off his face.

"The same," Simon replied with a smile. He paused while he paid for his order. "It's important," he added as he registered the detective's hesitation.

Peake shrugged. "Okay."

He knew his colleagues farther along the bar were taking an interest in the encounter and was equally aware that there could be some raised eyebrows among those who might have identified what the records described as a notorious criminal. But then he had long since given up worrying about appearances.

He nodded towards an empty table in the far corner of the saloon: "Over there."

"Thanks," said the Saint, and followed the detective through the crush of lunchtime drinkers.

Inspector Charlie Peake was one of the old school of police detectives. He had risen from a uniform through detective constable to detective sergeant and finally detective inspector. And there he would stay. Not because he lacked the ability or dedication to go higher, but because he did not fit into the training-college mould of smart young men currently favoured by the commissioners.

He wore a fawn trenchcoat that was in need of a visit to a dry cleaner's over a shiny and creased suit of blue serge. He was just over six feet with the breadth of shoulders and solid muscle to match his height. The toll of his job had added extra lines to the usual ones of middle age that etched the contours of his face. But it was the eyes which had held the Saint's attention. They were the heavy, permanently weary eyes of a man who has seen it all but who, despite everything, still cares.

They sat down, and the Saint declined the cigarette Peake offered. The detective lit one and spoke through the first cloud of smoke.

"So why is the famous Simon Templar interested in a small-time tea leaf like Owen?"

"I hear you've got him marked down for the robbery at St. Jude's," Simon said.

The detective's look was searching and there was a slightly harder edge to his voice.

"And how did you hear that exactly?"

"Father Bernardo is an old friend. He thinks you've got the wrong man and asked me to have a look at how things stand. Mind telling me what you've got on him?"

Peake puffed on his cigarette as he calculated how much he should reveal. He had long had a grudging respect for the man opposite, but the mere fact that it was the Saint who was asking made him immediately cautious and suspicious.

"I don't suppose it's classified," he admitted finally. "Owen has form, been in trouble since he was a kid. Minor stuff but consistent. Remand home, then Borstal, been clean since he came to London so far as we know anyway, but I suppose it was only a matter of time."

"Your faith in human nature is touching," Simon said cynically.

Peake shrugged.

"In my job I don't get much chance to practise it."

"But you've got to have a stronger case than just a criminal record."

Peake drained his glass, stubbed out his cigarette, and lit another.

"The robbery was an inside job, had to be. And that means it was Owen."

"Why?"

"Father Bernardo kept the chalice locked in a safe, a good one, and he never talked about it. Only he, his niece, and Owen knew it was there and so only one of them could have taken it. Oh, he tried to make it look like a break-in, even smashed a window from the outside, but he wasn't clever enough."

The Saint held back a smile and enquired with genuine interest: "Where did he go wrong?"

"The safe wasn't blown and it wasn't cut open, which means someone either used a key or picked the lock," Peake explained with the air of a senior officer lecturing a backward cadet. "There aren't more than half a dozen villains outside who could pick a lock like that, and they wouldn't bother unless they knew what it contained. That means it was opened with a key, and Owen knew where the keys were kept."

Simon mentally kicked himself for his professionalism, and knew as he did so that the criticism was undeserved because he had had no way of foreseeing what the sequel would be.

"Not only that," Peake continued in the same flat patient tone, "but when we pulled him in he had nearly a hundred pounds on him. He didn't get that kind of money helping Father Bernardo."

"What was his story?"

"Said he was saving up to get married and that he'd

had a bit of luck playing the horses. Then we asked him where he was last night and he says he went out to a movie and didn't meet anyone he knew to back the story up."

"It could just be true," Simon pointed out.

Peake allowed himself the excess of a short hard laugh.

"And I could become Chief Commissioner, but it isn't very likely, is it? If I had a pound for every time I've heard a story like that I wouldn't be worrying about how I'm going to live on my pension."

Simon had few doubts that a judge would be just as sceptical as the policeman.

"So you've charged him with stealing the chalice?"

Peake shook his head.

"Not yet. When we went to talk to him he tried to do a runner and bumped into a constable."

The Saint smiled thinly.

"Assaulting a police officer in the execution of his duty?"

"That's right. Just a holding charge so we can keep him safe while we sew up the evidence for the robbery."

The Saint considered the statement and his eyes brightened.

"Which is another way of saying that you haven't yet got a case that will stand up in court."

"We will have," Peake said confidently.

"Like to bet on it?" Simon asked.

"No." Peake pushed back his stool and stood up. He looked steadily down at the Saint. "And I don't want any meddling from you."

"Just offering to help the course of justice," said the Saint apologetically, as he too rose.

"Justice can get along without your help," Peake said, and made it sound like a warning.

Simon Templar's smile was never more enigmatic. "Too bad you're not a betting man," he mourned.

5

Simon Templar was by nature an optimist; it was simply not in character for him to remain downcast for long. Consequently the aura of despondency that had been eclipsing his halo during the morning was already thinning when he went in search of Charlie Peake. By the time he had left the pub, boarded a passing taxi, and directed the driver, it had almost completely evaporated.

So it was with a renewed sense of confidence that he relaxed in the back of the cab and appraised the situation.

Peake had said he could think of only six men outside prison capable of picklocking the safe. By the same standards, the number of fences equipped to handle the chalice was equally limited. There were many prepared to receive the everyday boodle of the everyday burglar, but only a handful possessed the specialist knowledge to value and dispose of such a distinctive work of art.

There was always the danger that the thief had passed it on to some back-street merchant to melt down for the scrap value of the metal and stones, but the Saint's renewed optimism refused to let him dwell for long on that possibility. One thing was certain: the mugger would try to get rid of the chalice as soon as he discovered that the violin case did not contain an easily pawnable violin.

The taxi stopped in one of the sheltered courts of

Gray's Inn. Simon paid off the driver and strolled through a brick-domed passageway into a small quadrangle. Although only a writ's throw away from some of the busiest of London's thoroughfares, the complex of age-mellowed buildings retained an air of more peaceful and leisurely days. Perhaps they lacked something of the quaintness of the Temple, where some of the last gas lamps in London still flickered, but they also embodied the feeling that the law, and lawyers, are not to be hurried.

He entered a building directly opposite the passageway and located the office he sought within the labyrinth of winding corridors. Robin Nash greeted his visitor with a ready smile and a firm handshake as soon as his secretary ushered the Saint into the room.

"Simon! Good to see you, it's been a long time," Nash said warmly, at last releasing the Saint's hand from his grip and indicating a chair. "I was beginning to think you'd taken a dislike to lawyers."

"Not to lawyers, just to the law," Simon said with a grin.

Robin Nash looked steadily at him, automatically estimating what was not apparent on the surface.

"Is this a social or a professional visit?" he asked after the brief scrutiny. "Are you in trouble again?"

"Professional. But I'm not in trouble."

"I'll believe the first answer and reserve my judgement on the second."

Simon laughed.

"There speaks the legal mind. But what can I expect from the best solicitor in London?"

"Flattery won't get you everything but it will win you a cup of tea."

He flicked a switch on the intercom and relayed the

order to his secretary. Simon, who had tasted the lawyer's own blend of Earl Grey before, was pleased.

Robin Nash sat back in his chair. He was a tall man in his early forties, hair receding at the temples and with a spreading waistline threatening to become a paunch. In sombre three-piece suit he looked what he was, one of the more successful solicitors in the capital. But there was also a certain strength to the shoulders and hands and an indefinably irreverent light behind the eyes which indicated that he had not spent all his life poring over dusty statute books. He had known the Saint well for more years than any legal practitioner conscious of the Bar's disciplinary council should freely admit.

Simon came to the point of his visit as soon as the tea was dispensed and the secretary had withdrawn.

"Tomorrow morning at Bow Street a kid called Taffy Owen comes up before the beak. The police are hanging a holding charge on him of assaulting a police officer. In fact they believe he stole a valuable antique chalice, but they haven't yet got all the evidence they need for a committal. I want you to represent him and get bail."

Nash considered the request for a time and then nodded.

"Okay. But why? What's your interest?"

"For the moment I can't tell you," Simon said. "Just leave it that I'm trying to prevent a miscarriage of justice."

Nash showed his scepticism at the reason with a dry smile.

"Sounds very noble. What about sureties?"

"I'll put up the money. Father Bernardo of St. Jude's Mission in Soho will promise the magistrates to keep an eye on him."

"The trouble is, Simon," the lawyer pointed out, "the magistrates may not consider you a very good risk. Your reputation would hardly commend you to them as a fit person to guarantee anybody's good behaviour."

"I don't want my name mentioned in court anyway. Tell them the money is being put up by Father Bernardo. And don't tell Taffy who really sprung him until he's outside. Then tell him if he wants real help to come and see me."

Nash considered the commission for a while in silence. Finally he shrugged.

"There's nothing in the rule book which says you have to tell me your motives. I'll consider myself hired."

Simon stood up.

"Thanks. Keep in touch."

Nash saw him to the door.

"You keep in touch. One of these days you may need a good attorney."

"Perhaps, when I write my will," said the Saint cheerfully.

As the office door closed behind him he looked at his watch. It showed a quarter past four.

At six o'clock J. J. Grondheim entered the lobby of the Savoy Hotel trailed by a porter carrying a large suitcase. The case, like its owner, was clearly well travelled. The labels plastered across it bore the names of many exotic destinations, while the scuffed leather along the sides showed that baggage handlers are the same the world over.

J. J. Grondheim wore no badge, but the reception clerk's experienced eye marked the new guest down as American before he had written a Los Angeles address in the register and listed his occupation as art dealer. Neither was Mr. Grondheim scuffed, being dressed in a precision-tailored lightweight grey suit only slightly creased by the long transatlantic flight. But there was a worldliness in his manner which suggested that he had seen the inside of more hotel rooms than the average chambermaid. He was comfortably over six feet, but the slight stoop of his broad shoulders made him appear shorter. His eyes were shielded by square horn-rimmed tinted glasses, and the black hair was heavily flecked with grey.

Once in his suite, he unpacked and arranged his clothes in wardrobe and chest and his toilet gear in the bathroom, indicating that he would be staying for at least a few days. That done, he went down to the bar and sank an old-fashioned at a corner table away from the main mob of customers before sauntering through to the Grill.

Again he chose a table apart from immediate neighbours and lingered over a Dover sole and a bottle of Muscadet. Returning at last to his room, he carefully rumpled the bedclothes so that the bed appeared to have been slept in and then, pocketing his key, made his way down by the stairs and left the hotel via the less-frequented Embankment exit.

J. J. Grondheim stood for a moment looking across at the reflection of the lights in the dark waters of the Thames, and took off his tinted glasses to reveal to no one a pair of wickedly clear blue eyes that could only have belonged to Simon Templar.

6

Vic Reefly was indexed in the Saint's mental data bank of villains under the umbrella heading "Racketeer." By the tax collector and the law-abiding populace generally he was believed to earn his comfortable living quite legally as owner of the Montparnasse Club in Frith Street.

Although it did not come within a champagne cork's flight of those select late-night pleasure domes in the quieter environs of Mayfair and Knightsbridge, the Montparnasse was still a rung above most of its competitors in Soho. The nightly takings kept his bank manager smiling, while the Vic Reefly Pension Fund was taken care of by a miscellany of extracurricular activities, most of which centred around detaching mugs from their money. None had so far been sufficiently poisonous to warrant the Saint's intervention, but Reefly was ambitious and the Saint maintained a watching brief.

It was Vic Reefly's boast that a rat couldn't sneeze between Piccadilly Circus and Tottenham Court Road without him hearing it.

Looking fresher and more elegant than anyone has a right to look in a night club at eleven-thirty in the morning, Simon Templar entered the Montparnasse with the sole intent of testing the claim. He descended the stairs from the front door into the reception lobby, where during business hours members were welcomed by a doorman whose physique was discreetly concealed by the cut of his dinner jacket. The experienced eye would also have noted that some of the waiters also appeared to have had more strenuous jobs in their time.

But at that hour the lobby was deserted and in the main room beyond there was only an elderly gent pushing a broom across the dance floor. Having long since learned that the key to good health lies in minding one's own business, he studiously attended to his sweeping and Simon was able to thread a path between the tables and enter unchallenged through a door beside the bar marked "Private."

Vic Reefly had been accused of many things but never of being beautiful. Unless (beauty being something in the beholder's eye) one was attracted to thickset men of average height with greased-down hair curling at the collar, who have more gold than enamel behind thin lips and a nose that appears to have once been remodelled by a heavy roller. Nor were the defects of his physiognomy redeemed by a sense of the sartorial. The yellow check suit, the black patent boots, and the wallpaper-patterned tie would not have won an award from the Tailors' Guild.

The Saint stood in the doorway, his gaze flitting around the cramped office and finally coming to rest on the ledger Reefly was scanning.

"Morning, Vic, cooking the books for breakfast?"

Vic Reefly looked up sharply and his eyes narrowed as they identified his visitor.

"Templar!" Surprise was quickly overtaken by suspicion. "What do you want?"

Simon closed the door and perched himself comfortably on the edge of the desk. He spent a moment attending to the crease of his trousers before replying.

"What I want, Victor, my little virus, is a word. Several, in fact."

Some of the tenseness eased out of the racketeer. He closed the ledger and sat back in his chair, but his eyes never left the Saint.

"What about?" he asked cautiously.

The Saint was not there to waste time, but he knew there would be no bonuses for seeming pressed for it.

"Oh, this and that," he answered with an airy wave of his hand. "A bit more this than that."

Once again his eyes roamed the room before returning to Reefly. And there was a light of dangerous devilment in them that made the racketeer's palms moisten.

"You know, Vic, there was a time when I might have paid you a less sociable visit," he said almost wistfully. "Especially after that little brannigan in Gerrard Street the other night."

The "little brannigan" had in fact been a sizeable melee in the course of which an illegal gambling club had been wrecked and its owner persuaded to part with the contents of his safe to pay the arrears on his "insurance."

"I hear the guy was breaking the law," Reefly said, with a faint twitch of his lips that might just have been meant for a smile.

"Whose law, Vic? Yours or the gentlemen's in blue?"

"Both," Reefly said curtly. "Now, Templar, if you ain't dropped in to pass the time of day, what can I do for you?"

Simon appeared to consider the question.

"It's more a question of what I can do for you," he said at last. "There was a break-in at St. Jude's the other night. A certain article was stolen. I'm interested in it."

Reefly nodded thoughtfully.

"I heard about it," he said guardedly. "What's your interest?"

"That's my business," the Saint answered briskly. "Let's just say that if you put me in touch with the right party you wouldn't lose on the deal—and neither would they."

The racketeer pondered the request for a while and seemed to find something amusing in it. When the Saint entered he had expected trouble, now it looked as if

Simon Templar would owe him a favour, and he knew just how valuable an asset that could be.

He grinned, displaying his expensively gilded teeth.

"It might be arranged," he conceded warily. "I'll see what can be done."

"You do that, Vic," said the Saint, and stood up.

He stopped as he reached the door.

"And do it soon." He smiled, but Reefly found nothing reassuring in the sight. "I'd hate to have to pay a less friendly visit."

He left the club with a vague feeling of annoyance. He disliked Reefly and his kind on principle and was not happy with the possibility of becoming indebted to him. But that was a price about which he might not be able to haggle.

At the same time as he was climbing into a taxi and directing the driver to Upper Berkeley Mews, Taffy Owen was stepping from the dock at Bow Street. The unexpected appearance of Robin Nash had turned what the police solicitor had expected to be a straightforward remand in custody into a legal wrangle in which he was soon floundering. The magistrates were impressed by such a prominent advocate and his arguments, and Father Bernardo's character reference together with a hefty financial deposit had combined to win Owen the bail the Saint wanted.

Simon was finishing a light lunch of smoked salmon, brown bread, and a bottle of Muscadet when his doorbell sounded.

He opened the door to admit Mila and a youth whom she introduced as Taffy, bade them welcome, sat them down, and dispensed coffee while listening to Mila's account of the hearing.

He waved aside her thanks as he deposited himself in a chair facing Owen, whom he regarded with dispassionate appraisal.

"Okay, son," he invited softly. "Tell Uncle Simon the story of your life."

Taffy Owen could not have been much older than twenty, and although he was almost as tall as the Saint he was slim to the point of thinness. His curly black hair had not come in contact with a brush that day, and he appeared not to have shaved for twice as long. His jacket and trousers had been new a long time before he acquired them, and the cheap open-necked shirt looked as if it had been slept in.

He nervously avoided looking directly at Simon. He glanced around the room like an animal searching for an escape route, but the elegant and expensive furnishings he saw only served to increase his discomfort. Eventually he contented himself with staring at the pattern on the carpet.

Simon waited patiently for the boy to begin his story, but when at last he spoke it hardly amounted to a speech.

"I didn't do it," he mumbled.

The Saint sighed.

"Okay, just for a moment we'll take that as read. But remember, I'm the guy who's keeping you out of the slammer, and if I'm to continue to do that I'll need some answers. Where were you while the chalice was being stolen?"

"I went for a walk," Taffy said wearily. "I've already told it all to the police."

"So tell me too," said the Saint. "What did you do? And how come you had so much money on you?"

Taffy sat back in his chair and for the first time looked

straight at the Saint. He spoke as if reciting a lesson learned by rote.

"About ten I left the mission and went for a walk. I had a drink in a pub near Trafalgar Square but the barman doesn't remember me. Then I walked up through Green Park to Piccadilly and from there to St. Jude's. I got back around midnight and went straight to bed. I just wanted some fresh air. I can't prove it but it's true." Owen spread his hands in a gesture of despair. "Look, if I really had taken the chalice, don't you think I'd have a better alibi than that?"

"Depends whether you are very stupid or very clever," Simon said. "Go on."

Taffy shrugged.

"That's it. I was having breakfast when they came and pulled me in."

"And how did you come by that hundred quid?"

"That was his savings," said Mila quickly. "We're planning to get married."

"So you knew he had the money?"

Mila looked uncertainly from Taffy to the Saint.

"Well, no, I didn't know he had so much," she admitted. "But I knew Taffy had been doing odd jobs to get some."

"I wanted to buy an engagement ring," Owen said. "It was going to be a surprise."

Mila slipped her arm through his and squeezed it affectionately. The look in her eyes said more about her feelings for Taffy than her words could ever have done.

Simon considered the story objectively. As he had pointed out to Peake, it could all be true but, even hearing it from Taffy personally, he could not dissociate himself from the detective's scepticism. It could not be proved but neither could it be disproved, and the measure of doubt might give Owen an edge with a judge and jury. The Saint wanted it to be true for Mila's sake. But for just that reason he had to be certain. He realised that trying to break such a non-alibi was futile, and questioning about the lad's trouble in the past would only create a barrier of hostility.

He changed tack.

"So, Taffy, if you didn't steal the chalice who did?"

It was a loaded question, for whoever had stolen it the second time might know that it was the Saint himself who had lifted it first. He searched the other's face for any hint that the shot had scored, but he might just as well have studied a wooden mask—or the rehearsed expression of a good actor.

Taffy rebounded the question in a flat, tired tone without giving a clue to whether the reply was also double-edged.

"You're the famous detective. You tell me."

Simon smiled thoughtfully.

"Well, that's what we have to find out," he said blandly.

"What's puzzling me," said Mila, unaware of the verbal fencing match she was interrupting, "is how the thief thinks he's ever going to be able to sell the chalice. I mean, it's not the sort of thing you can just go into a pawnshop and put on the counter."

"There are ways," Simon said briefly; and then, realising a new avenue was opening before him, went on: "My guess is he passed it on to a fence, probably taking a deposit, with the balance to come when the receiver has placed it."

"But surely the fence would still have trouble getting rid of it," Taffy said.

The Saint continued to watch him closely while he explained.

"There are specialist dealers around who work for very rich and very unscrupulous collectors, people who keep their treasures in vaults and gloat over them in private. I happen to know that there's one of those operators in London right now. A character named Grondheim, staying at the Savoy and in the market for anything that's not on general sale."

The Saint's tone was deliberately casual. A professional outlining tricks of the trade to the uninitiated. But the words were carefully chosen. They formed the trip wire of the trap he had begun to build the previous evening. Now all that remained was to wait and see who walked into it.

7

Vic Reefly did not believe in wasting time, and he started doing what he had been asked to do even before Simon Templar closed the front door of the Montparnasse Club behind him. But he was not a miracle worker, as he pointed out forcefully when the Saint telephoned later the same afternoon.

"I know you don't perform miracles, Vic," Simon agreed soothingly. "If you did, those bottles of water behind the bar might turn into alcohol. I just wondered how you were getting on."

"None the quicker for you asking," Reefly answered

sourly. "I've put out some feelers and I think we'll get something pretty soon. How do I contact you?"

"I'm staying at the Savoy while my place is redecorated. Ask for Mr. Tombs. Got that?"

"Sure I've got it," said Reefly testily. "Tombs, eh? What's your game, Saint?"

"I'll teach it to you someday, Vic," Simon replied with a laugh. "But the rules are a bit complicated."

He dropped the receiver into its cradle and lay back on the bed, gazing at the white plaster ceiling of the hotel room and resigning himself to a period of patient waiting.

Mila and Taffy had left Upper Berkeley Mews a short while after he had told them about J. J. Grondheim. Had they loitered outside for half an hour, they would have been surprised to see that same American gentleman emerge from the premises and take a cab to the hotel. Had Vic Reefly been in the lobby of the Savoy when the said Mr. Grondheim returned, he might have been equally surprised to hear him tell the receptionist that any calls for a Mr. Sebastian Tombs, an English business colleague, were to be put through to his suite.

With the hook well and truly baited there was nothing left to do but sit at the other end of the line and wait for a bite. He could not leave the hotel in case a call came, and so he whiled away the evening with a long and very expensive dinner followed by a sojourn in the bar where he discussed the rising crime rate in New York with a Manhattan advertising executive who was surprised by the breadth of his comprehensive knowledge of the subject.

At breakfast the following morning he was supplied with all the daily papers to help him pass the time. He had consigned three to the wastepaper basket before his telephone rang. The operator informed him that a gentleman named Dankin was asking to see him. The Saint told her to send him up.

Mr. Jonathan Dankin aptly fitted the description "gentleman." He was slightly built, with a dapper taste in suits and a penchant for brightly coloured shirts. He carried himself with an assurance and spoke with an accent that identified him as a product of one of the better public schools. Anyone meeting him for the first time would not have been surprised to discover that he ran an antique shop in the Fulham Road, though they might have thought that Bond Street would have seemed a more fitting location.

Mr. Dankin would have agreed with them, but the firm of auctioneers in that particular thoroughfare for whom he had once worked would most certainly not have done so. They had dispensed with his services upon discovering that the works of art he declared copies, and so worth a fraction of their apparent value when under the hammer, were really originals. How many had been bought by Dankin's accomplice at a knockdown price and later sold for considerably more had never been sorted out. His distinguished employers had not wanted to undergo the scandal of a formal investigation. Jonathan Dankin had left quietly to set up in business on his own.

The word was put round the antiques trade that he was not to be trusted. But what is a bad reputation in one quarter can amount to a testimonial in another. His specialist knowledge brought him many lucrative commissions, and as he knocked on the door of the Saint's room he had few doubts that his present errand would be any exception.

Simon Templar had heard of Dankin though they had never met. In the circles in which the Saint moved, the fence was referred to not by his baptismal name but by the title conferred by those who visited his premises only at night: "the Professor"—commonly abbreviated to "the Prof."

As soon as Simon opened the door the Prof produced a visiting card from his waistcoat pocket and handed it over. It stated simply his name and occupation, and carried a phone number without an address.

"I understand that you are in the same business, Mr. Grondheim," Dankin said.

The Saint looked from the card to the dealer. His face was expressionless.

"Maybe," he agreed warily. "Come in and we'll talk about it."

"Do you come to London often?" Dankin enquired as the Saint led the way into the sitting room.

"Sometimes," Simon said, motioning Dankin to a chair. "But I don't think we've ever met."

"Well, better late than never."

The Saint sat opposite, conscious that he was being examined but confident that his cover would pass any test Dankin could impose.

"How did you know about me?" Simon asked.

"One hears these things, you know," Dankin said. "One makes it one's business to, you understand. Contacts in the trade, and with the staff in hotels such as this, for instance. Word gets around."

"Really," drawled the Saint. "And what did the word tell you, Mr. Dankin?"

"That you may be in the market for certain merchandise not, shall we say, on public display."

"Is that so?" said the Saint slowly. "You'll appreciate, Mr. Dankin, that as I don't know you I should like some sort of reference. Don't get me wrong, but I'm sure you'll understand if I'd like to check with the person who sent you."

The Professor looked at him without speaking for several seconds. He had been in such situations before and knew how to deal with them. He allowed the Saint to know he was being scrutinised and then leisurely rose to his feet.

"It appears, Mr. Grondheim, that I may have been misinformed." His tone was brisk, almost curt. "I won't take up any more of your time."

The Saint never moved from his chair. He knew that Dankin had little intention of leaving, but the card had been skilfully played and deserved to take the trick if not the game.

"Sit down, Mr. Dankin," he said with a brief smile. "A man in my position has to be careful."

The Prof returned the smile as he resumed his seat.

"We all have to be careful, Mr. Grondheim," he agreed. "Now perhaps we can talk business."

"Sure. What are you offering?"

"There are a number of items available to someone like yourself at the moment, Mr. Grondheim, but none, I think, which quite matches this."

Dankin took a small black and white photograph from the inside pocket of his coat and held it out.

"If you are interested I could of course arrange an actual examination," he continued, but the Saint barely heard him.

What he did hear as he gazed at the snapshot of the chalice was the whirring of imaginary gears as the wire was tripped and the trap began to close.

8

Simon appeared to study the photograph closely for half a minute before speaking.

"Middle eighteenth century . . . Evidence of Florentine influence, but the detail appears somewhat crude and heavy. Could be Portuguese but more probably Spanish," he pronounced, and handed back the picture.

The Prof nodded approvingly.

"I see you know your antiques, Mr. Grondheim."

"I know my job," Simon responded, allowing a new curtness into his voice.

In its own way it was the truest statement he had made that morning. During a lifetime of wide-ranging piracy he had been obliged to learn to evaluate many exotic forms of plunder.

"You would like to view?" enquired the Prof, as he slipped the photograph back into his pocket.

"I would like to view," the Saint said, and paused momentarily before adding: "When would you like to bring it here?"

Mr. Dankin seemed slightly shocked by the suggestion.

"To the hotel? Come now, Mr. Grondheim, I'm surprised you should even ask such a question."

The Saint's sigh carried just the right pitch of professional resignation.

"It's only that I'm a little tired of midnight meetings in back rooms."

He had not expected Dankin to agree, but it had been worth asking on the off chance. He knew the formalities that had to be observed on such occasions. The pattern dictated that they would haggle over the price; that a price would be agreed; that he would be taken to see the chalice, and that he would hand over the cash. Thus ran the conventional scenario. But the Saint had never considered himself bound by any scenario, and he had his own notion of the way in which the rules of the game might eventually be interpreted. For the present, however, there was nothing he could do but tag along with whatever arrangements the Prof felt like making.

"Your price?" Simon asked.

The Prof thought for a few seconds.

"Let us say thirty thousand pounds," he suggested, with the air of a man anxious to be helpful even at cost to himself.

The Saint smiled thinly.

"Let's say fifteen."

The Prof appeared startled, as if he had been suddenly and unexpectedly insulted.

The bartering continued along well-worn grooves until they compromised on twenty-four thousand pounds, a figure both men knew to be about the chalice's actual value on a high-class thieves' market.

"Do you want pounds, dollars, or Swiss francs?" Simon asked when the figure had been agreed on.

"Sterling will be quite acceptable, thank you," said the Prof primly, and stood up. "I will telephone this afternoon, when you will have had time to obtain the cash. I'm sure we can get our business concluded well before midnight."

The Saint returned the smile with a grin equally lacking in warmth.

"Yes," he agreed softly as he heard the outer door of the suite close behind the fence. "Yes, I'm sure we can."

After a boringly lazy day spent mostly within the confines of the hotel he received the promised call shortly after five. The instructions were simple and direct. If Mr. Grondheim was in the middle of Waterloo Bridge, on the east side, with the money, at ten, he would be taken to see the chalice.

The choice of location showed a professionalism that Simon Templar appreciated. Cars do not normally park on bridges, therefore any that were would immediately arouse the suspicions of whoever arrived to collect him. Therefore the chances of his arranging to be followed were greatly reduced.

He was duly on the said bridge at the appointed time, with a briefcase in hand, and when a car pulled into the kerb beside him he spared it only one searching glance before climbing in beside the driver.

It was a black production-line saloon, indistinguishable from a thousand others traversing the streets of London that night, except that the acceleration of their departure showed that the engine had been made capable of a degree of performance far beyond the advertised claims of the manufacturer.

To the uninitiated the action of Mr. Grondheim in getting into a strange car in a strange city while carrying a considerable amount of instantly spendable currency might have appeared more than a little foolhardy. But then the uninitiated, by definition, do not know the protocol of such transactions. That Mr. Grondheim might easily have been forced to part with his money without ever getting a glimpse of the object it was to be spent on is true, but it is equally certain that had that happened the Prof would never have sold another stolen artifact, because a leper would have been treated as an honoured guest compared to the reception he would have received among his peers. It was also probable that some very large men would have been knocking at his door very shortly afterwards.

By the same token, Mr. Grondheim might have relieved the Prof of the chalice and refused to hand over the money. But Mr. Grondheim would be aware that his chances of leaving the country, or even London, with his money, the chalice, and himself intact would have been equal to the survival rating of a three-legged mouse in a cattery.

It was not honour among thieves. It was simply an understanding based on a mutual instinct for survival.

The only danger lay in the unlikely event of Mr. Grondheim not really being an accepted member of the brotherhood, which was why the Saint got into the car with only a tiny tremor of unease.

The driver was the only other occupant of the car. Simon's chatty "Where to?" as they shot away received no reply, and other efforts to enliven the conversation during the drive were equally unsuccessful.

The man was in his mid-thirties and powerfully proportioned, but with a degree of intelligence in his features which indicated that he was not solely employed for his physical prowess. In the lexicon of the underworld, he was a "minder"—a cross between a bodyguard, a chauffeur, and an aide-de-camp.

Had the Saint really been a visiting American and not a native of the city with a knowledge of its byways that would have shamed a taxi driver, he would most certainly have been lost within the first half mile.

They headed south and toured the back streets around the Elephant and Castle before recrossing the river via

Victoria Bridge. A meander through Belgravia followed until they hit Kensington, and the driver, finally convinced that they were not being shadowed, swung the car through the gates of Hyde Park. Their journey ended in the car park behind the restaurant near the Serpentine. The tarmac expanse was bare except for a Rolls-Royce in the far corner. They parked a few yards from it.

The driver half turned in his seat and jerked his head to indicate that his passenger should alight. As the Saint swung himself onto the ground the driver also got out and came around the car. He kept one hand in his coat pocket as his other patted the Saint's clothes. Satisfied as to the absence of artillery, he nodded towards the Rolls and fell into step, a pace to the rear, as the Saint walked towards it.

Mr. Jonathan Dankin was sitting in the corner of the back seat. He switched on the interior light as the Saint climbed in and settled himself in the other corner. The driver remained outside, but so close that his frame blocked the window. Simon looked from the minder to Dankin.

"I see you don't believe in taking chances," he observed approvingly, and the Prof again gave his impression of a smile.

"In our business, Mr. Grondheim, one can't afford to. Do you have the money?"

"Naturally."

Simon opened the briefcase, on his knees, and permitted the Prof a glimpse of the neatly packed bundles of currency it contained.

His own gaze rested on the violin case which lay on the seat between them. Understanding the meaning of his look, the Prof flicked up the catches and took out the chalice, handing it across as casually as if he had been offering his guest a cigarette.

The Saint held the chalice in both hands and smiled. He inspected it for a few seconds, just to make sure that it was the genuine article and not a hastily manufactured substitute, and then faced Dankin squarely.

"Just what I've been looking for," he stated with absolute honesty.

The Prof smiled.

"Then it's a deal?"

The Saint slowly shook his head, and when he spoke again there was no longer any trace of his former accent.

"I'm afraid, Prof, my little parasite, that you have been had, well and truly, one hundred per cent taken for the proverbial ride," he explained softly. "You see, this chalice means a lot to a very dear friend of mine and I'm committed to returning it to him, and I've already gone to considerable expense to locate it."

Dankin stared at his client while the words registered their meaning and then he opened his mouth to shout. The Saint did nothing to stop him. While he was speaking he had released the door catch and at the same time carefully placed the sole of his left shoe flat against the panel halfway between window and floor.

The Prof shouted and the minder outside turned and the Saint straightened his leg. The heavy door flew open and its edge caught the bodyguard flush in the centre of his chest and sent him reeling back. Before he could completely regain his balance the Saint was out of the car.

It is doubtful if the minder ever understood the precise sequence of the events which followed. One instant he felt himself stumbling backwards, his arms flailing as he attempted to remain vertical. Then he stopped retreating as two clamps appeared to fasten themselves on his collar and belt, and then he was flying back towards the car. Very soon afterwards his head made contact with the ground on the far side of the Rolls, and then he slept.

The Prof was still gaping out of the opposite window at his slumbering employee when the Saint leaned in and retrieved his briefcase and the violin case from the seat beside him. Dankin jerked round, instinctively cowering at the movement, but making only a feeble attempt to prevent it.

"You'll never get away with this," he said furiously.

The Saint laughed.

"I wish I had a tenner for every time someone has said that to me," he remarked, and then his tone became serious. "One last thing, Prof, and I'll be on my way. Who sold you the chalice?"

Simon waited for an answer but Dankin only goggled at him. It was a brace of seconds before the Saint realised that the fence was not looking at him but past him. In that same moment he heard the rustle of grass and spun round just in time to meet the first of the trio of men who had sprung from the bushes beside the kerb.

9

The pundit who proclaimed that when history repeats itself the first time it is tragedy and the second farce was commenting on weightier matters than an attempt at grievous bodily harm, but that does not make the pronouncement any less applicable.

This adventure had opened with the robber robbed,

and the clear intention of the three heavies now bearing down on the Saint was to top it in exactly the same manner. The first occasion had threatened tragedy for Father Bernardo, the mission in general, and Taffy Owen in particular. The second might turn out to be farce but, Simon decided, it would be he who did the laughing.

This time too there was a difference. The Saint saw the attack coming and after the frustrations of the preceding days he would have happily taken on double the opposition purely for the pleasure of the exercise.

They came in a ragged line, the man in the centre a pace ahead of his companions. He wore a precision-tailored dinner jacket and spotless patents, his face was freshly scrubbed, and not one slicked-down hair was out of place. He looked as if he belonged on a dance floor rather than on a battleground, and he could hardly have presented a greater contrast to his companions.

The one to his right was thin-faced, a head shorter, and his rattish features were a day overdue for a shave. The third member of the party towered over them all, with a head like a boulder perched on shoulders like cliffs. They were known to their peers by the handles of Dandy, Slasher, and Bull.

The Saint recognised them; and their presence answered a question that had been bothering him since the previous morning. Now, untroubled, there was nothing else to do but enjoy the fun.

Dandy was within striking distance a fraction of a second after Simon completed his turn, and the two feet of lead pipe he carried was already swishing the air in the direction of the Saint's cranium. That it dented the roof of the Rolls and not its target was solely due to a co-ordinated flow of reflex actions which sent the Saint earthwards as fast as if a trap door had opened beneath him. When he had descended as far as he could he came up again with the velocity of a howitzer shell.

Having missed at the first attempt, the speed of the Saint's counter allowed him no margin for a second. The top of the Saint's forehead exploded beneath his chin, and as Simon continued upwards his attacker began to go down. And that, simply and undramatically, was that.

Bull and Slasher now closed in from either side, but the Saint did not wait to receive them. Instead he went forward, jumping nimbly over the still crumpling Dandy and turning in the air as he went. Confused, both men halted and hesitated; the Saint did not. He sidestepped to his right, so placing the now prone figure of Dandy between himself and Bull. The move gave him invaluable seconds in which to concentrate on the smallest member of the committee.

As a straight opponent, the little man would have been an outside bet if the Saint had had his leg in plaster. But the cutthroat razor which glinted in his hand lowered the odds considerably.

Simon had no desire for what is termed in that locality a "Soho facial," and there was an experienced air about the way the razor was held which inferred that Slasher was quite accustomed to providing such cosmetic surgery.

With Bull beginning to lumber forward to his left and the razor merchant beginning to advance behind his blade directly ahead, the Saint moved to his right. It was a situation the Marquis of Queensberry had not legislated for, and in such circumstances the Saint considered that the belt should be worn around the knees.

His foot travelled upwards and his leg straightened as his toe thudded into the little man's groin. Slasher screamed, and the razor slipped from his fingers as he doubled over. The Saint stepped in swiftly and his fist slammed up into the thug's face with a force that sent him sprawling backwards to land in a writhing heap at Bull's feet.

Bull carried no weapon simply because he had always found that his physique made them unnecessary. He charged into the attack in a worthy imitation of his namesake. Any of his flailing punches would have ended the fight immediately had it connected, but the Saint was careful to ensure that they did not connect. He was giving away two inches in height and roughly eighty pounds in weight, and if he did not respect the man's skill as a boxer he respected the physical differences.

Simon met Bull's first attack with a barrage of straight jabs to the head that stopped him in his tracks. The tough replied by lashing out with his foot, but the Saint swayed to one side and took advantage of his opponent's momentary loss of balance to drive home a combination of blows to the ribs that made Bull wince and reel away. The man was so large, and his technique so rudimentary, that for a trained fighter he was an almost impossible target to miss.

The Saint advanced behind a left hand that licked out and stung quicker than a snake's tongue. Bull's counters, such as they were, were absorbed by the bunched muscles of the Saint's arms and shoulders, whose continual ducking and weaving meant that those that did get through were mainly glancing blows with little power left in them.

A final crunching left hook cracked home high on the side of the bruiser's battered face and he stopped backtracking. His arms sagged and his eyes glazed, and he began to rock unsteadily. It is unlikely that he ever saw the uppercut that finally dropped him in front of the Rolls.

The whole affair was over in far less than the time taken to read about it. The Prof had watched from the safety of the Rolls, as transfixed as a rabbit in the beam of a searchlight. Only when Bull disappeared from his view did he suddenly realise his own danger, and by then it was too late.

The Saint's hand descended on him before he had covered a dozen yards, and their conversation was resumed.

"I swear, I didn't know they were there. Honest, you have to believe me," Dankin blubbered as he was pushed roughly back against the side of the car.

"I'm sure you swear and I'm absolutely certain you're not honest," Simon replied. "But I do believe you."

Relief showed itself by adding a faint tint to the fence's ashen face, and then he looked into the clear cold blue of the Saint's eyes and the colour faded again.

"You and your playmates have put me to a great deal of trouble," said the Saint, and the dispassionate evenness of his voice was more menacing than any threats could have been.

He was about to elaborate on the theme, but the sounds emanating from the razor merchant indicated that the nausea which had rendered him useless was passing, and a low moan from the far side of the car showed that an earlier victim was also returning to an awareness of his surroundings.

The Saint smiled.

"Now you can help me. Open the door."

The Prof obediently opened the rear door of the Rolls, and the Saint placed one hand on Slasher's collar and the other on the seat of his pants and tossed him through the opening.

Around the other side, Dankin's minder was just pulling himself upright but was too groggy to object as the Saint repeated the performance on his person. With the Prof's help, Simon bundled first Dandy and then Bull into the car. The impact of the two unconscious thugs on top of the two already struggling to untangle their respective arms and legs was sufficiently deadening and confusing to allow the Saint the amount of time he required.

He removed the keys from the ignition and opened the rear compartment. He beckoned to the Prof.

"In."

Dankin looked from the dark cavern to the Saint.

"But . . ."

"In," Simon repeated, and the Prof, because there was nothing else he could do, obeyed.

Simon banged the lid shut and strode quickly to the car that had brought him. Its equipment did not contain the tow rope he had hoped for, but there was a very comprehensive tool kit. He selected a heavy hammer and returned to the Rolls. He opened the near-side rear door, pushed the catch to lock, and then brought the hammer down with the full strength of his arm behind it. The metal sheered off, and the Saint slammed the door and tested that it was secure before repeating the operation on the other three exits.

He stood back and surveyed his handiwork. It was not the most secure of prisons but, as two of its occupants would be sleeping for some time, and as the freedom of movement of the other pair was further restricted by the thick glass which partitioned the front seats from the rear, he judged it would hold long enough.

As he walked back to the other car his foot struck against something metal which on examination proved to be a .38 automatic. It must have fallen from Dankin's bodyguard's pocket during his flight, and with a faint smile the Saint thoughtfully slipped it into his own before swinging himself behind the wheel and gunning the engine into life. He swung the saloon in an arc and headed back onto the main road around the park that would bring him out near Marble Arch.

At a call box in Oxford Street he dialled the number of C Division and requested to speak to Detective Inspector Peake. He looked at his watch while he waited to be put through. It needed a few minutes to eleven. Fortunately the detective was still at his desk. He did not, however, sound particularly pleased when his caller identified himself.

"What do you want, Templar?" he demanded gruffly.

"I'm doing my law-abiding citizen act," Simon told him. "It's very popular—packs 'em in at the Palladium and the Chipping Gooseberry police ball. Death-defying feats of honesty, breathtaking bouts of truthfulness, dazzling displays of decency. You must catch my next spectacular, all profits to the fund for research into putting brains under policemen's helmets."

Peake was unimpressed.

"Very amusing if you happen to like listening to drivel at this time of night. I don't, so say what you called to say."

"You have no sense of the absurd, Inspector," Simon remonstrated sadly. "Me, now, I have got a sense of the absurd, and I find it highly amusing that at this moment four of Vic Reefly's heavy mob are locked in a Rolls-Royce behind the restaurant in Hyde Park and that their luggage in the back consists of a fence you've wanted to nail for years. Are you laughing yet?"

"No, but I'm interested."

"Well, I advise you to toddle over fairly rapidly before they commit criminal damage to the interior of the said Rolls in trying to get out. Also I'm not sure how much air the poor old Prof has to spare. Personally, I don't fancy giving him the kiss of life, but if the idea turns you on . . ."

"I'm on my way," Peake cut in. "You will be there?"

"'Fraid not, Charlie. You can have the tiddlers. I've got a bigger fish to fry."

"Listen, Saint, if you . . ."

But the Saint was not listening. He dropped the receiver into its bracket, got back into the car, which was now loaded with the violin case and his own attaché case, and pointed the radiator towards Soho.

10

Vic Reefly was not of a nervous disposition at any time, and in his office, with a quick escape route to the shop above via a trap door in the ceiling and a bevy of muscular employees outside, he felt at his most secure. So much so that he did not even bother to see what the fuss was about when the crash of glass and the thud of toppling tables reached him. At that time of night there were often fights and, far from objecting, the patrons welcomed them as part of the floor show. The noise subsided, and when the door opened he expected to hear only a brief report of the damage.

What he heard that night was a mocking drawling voice that seemed to lower the temperature of his blood by about sixty degrees Fahrenheit.

"What cheer, Victor. I was just passing so I thought I'd drop in. Unfortunately I seem to have landed on some of your staff."

Reefly froze. He was kneeling beside the safe in the corner of the room with his back to the door when the Saint entered, and for several seconds seemed incapable of movement. When he did stir it was to send his hand darting towards the back of the safe.

"Don't be silly, Vic," cautioned the Saint.

Simultaneously Reefly recognised both the click of a safety catch being flicked and the sense of the Saint's words. He withdrew his hand. Slowly he stood up and turned. The Saint was sitting on the edge of the table opposite the desk just as he had the previous morning, except that this time he was holding a .38 automatic.

"Sit down, chum, and let words pass between us," Simon instructed, and Reefly did as he was told. "I'm afraid I've done some damage to your furniture and even more to two of your waiters who seemed to think you didn't want to be disturbed. I didn't expect it to be quite so easy, but then your regiment was under strength, what with your doorman, your barman, and your pet gorilla being otherwise engaged."

"What have you done with them?"

The Saint smiled briefly as if he found a passing memory amusing.

"Not as much as I would have liked to do. But it was fun while it lasted."

Reefly said nothing because there was nothing he could say. He had been in the game long enough to know when to throw in his hand. His best tactic now was just to keep silent and improvise when the chance came.

Simon Templar was happy to accept the stage. His tone was conversational, but the business end of the .38 never wavered from its target between the third and fourth buttons of Reefly's flowery waistcoat.

"I suppose it wasn't a bad idea from your point of view," he conceded. "You tell the Prof about a possible buyer, you find out where the meet is going to be and arrange for a reception committee. That way you not only get to keep the chalice and the money but you get rid of me. Not permanently, of course, that would have caused too much fuss, but you figured that even I would have difficulty exacting my revenge with both legs in traction. And while I was out of action you could get on with those ambitious little schemes I warned you about yesterday. Correct?"

Reefly stage-managed a shrug.

"You're the one who's doing the talking."

He tried to sound offhand but his mouth was too dry and his throat too tight to achieve the proper insouciant inflection.

Simon beamed across at Reefly.

"Don't I sound interesting? It would have been a great scheme if it had worked—but unfortunately for you it didn't."

"So what are you going to do about it? You can't use that popgun of yours in here."

"What am I going to do about it?" echoed the Saint, as if considering the question for the first time. "Well, let's consider the options. They're building a new flyover at Kew and you could always help prop it up. No, I've done something similar to that before, and I do try not to repeat myself."

He paused for a moment and in the silence Reefly seemed to hear his own heart beating.

"I could feed you to the jackals at the London Zoo, but I hear they're a bit particular about the quality of their diet," Simon said at last. "Then again there's always the traditional cement booties and a swim down to Greenwich, but I hear they're trying to clean the pollution from the Thames and I'd hate to add to their problems." He sighed. "So I suppose it's just going to have to be prison. Not very original and even less personally satisfying, but I'm getting so damned respectable these days."

Reefly stared as if he could not believe his ears. And then he laughed.

"The police?" he demanded incredulously. "You're going to go to the law and tell them I tried to nick a stolen chalice from you? They'd run you in as fast as me."

The Saint shook his head, and that simple movement drained Reefly of all his suddenly found confidence.

"I'm afraid you've got it all wrong, Vic. Right now, Inspector Peake is picking up what's left of your enforcement squad, plus the Prof. And Brother Dankin at least is sure to sing, even if the others don't. He'll tell them that you sold him the chalice. So you're going to admit you stole it."

"Like hell I am," said Reefly from between clenched teeth.

"Oh yes, you are, dear heart," Simon corrected. "Because if you don't, I'm going to give Peake a complete rundown on all the little gems of information I've collected about you over the years. Admit you stole the chalice and you'll go down for five years and be out in three with remission. Refuse, and by the time I'm finished they'll be throwing away the keys."

Silence ensued while Reefly considered his options and made the choice the Saint had known he would have to make. Finally he nodded.

"I thought you'd see it my way," said the Saint. "Two more things. First, who really brought you the chalice?"

The answer was the one Simon had expected but he felt no pleasure in having been proved right. He stood up and crossed the room.

"Second, this has been a rather expensive business so I'm sure you won't mind contributing to my expenses."

Reefly watched sullenly as the Saint knelt by the safe and extracted the wads of banknotes he had placed inside it a few minutes earlier. Simon stuffed the money into his jacket pockets. At a rough guess he put the total at around three thousand pounds. He wiped the door clean of his fingerprints, closed it on Reefly's gun, and spun the dial.

"Bye, Vic. I'll think of you every time I have porridge for breakfast." He stopped at the door and turned. "You may think about trying to double-cross me. Try it and I guarantee you'll never think about anything again."

11

The chalice stood in the centre of Father Bernardo's desk. Even minus its ornate lid, which the Saint had left in the Rolls beside the Prof to support the story he had built, it looked imposing, but to the Saint somehow less beautiful than when he had first seen it in that same room such a short while before.

He had just recounted the full story to the pastor and his niece—or almost the full story. Father Bernardo looked steadily at the chalice and said wearily: "I am happy it has been returned, even if now we again have the problem of keeping St. Jude's open."

Simon produced the banknotes he had lifted from Vic Reefly's safe not very long before.

"A donation," he said.

"From you?" asked Mila. "But we couldn't—"

The Saint shook his head and smiled.

"No, not from me, from Vic Reefly. He experienced his own road to Damascus—or should it be Dartmoor?"

"There is one thing you have not told us," said Father Bernardo. "Who really stole the chalice?"

It was the question Simon had been dreading, but fate decided that he would not have to answer it.

At that moment the study door opened and Taffy Owen stepped into the room. He saw the chalice and stopped, hesitated for a moment as he looked into the three faces turned towards him, and then turned and ran.

They listened in silence as his steps thudded on the uncarpeted stairs. The Saint made no attempt to follow him. Presently the front door slammed.

Simon looked at Mila and understood the effort she was making to hold back her tears. Father Bernardo studied his hands.

"He must have heard us discussing stealing the chalice. It was easy for him to slip out, hide, and cosh me as I climbed down the drainpipe. He took it straight to Reefly, and that's how he came by the hundred pounds the police found. I'm sorry, Mila."

The girl said nothing but rose shakily to her feet and walked out of the room.

Father Bernardo looked at the Saint.

"So what do we do now?" he asked wearily.

"We do nothing," Simon said. "If we tell the police that Taffy stole the chalice, then he's going to point the finger at me because I stole it in the first place, and if that happens you're going to be dragged in as an accomplice. Anyway, it would only mean prolonging the misery for Mila."

"Then Taffy gets away with it," said Father Bernardo. "It doesn't seem right."

"It's not," Simon admitted. "But that kid hasn't got the brains to stay out of trouble for long, and next time he won't be so lucky. At least you won't be seeing him around here any more."

"You know, I really thought he had changed," said Father Bernardo. "I thought that I—we had changed him."

"Like the man said, you can't win 'em all," said the Saint. "What is important is that you don't stop trying."

"You are right of course," Father Bernardo said. And then he smiled. "But then, as a priest, how could I disagree with a Saint?"

II

The Unsaintly Santa

1

There is an art to the making of mulled ale. The beer should be strong and dark but not too bitter. A steady hand should add the cloves, and the nutmeg should be little more than a suggestion. The brew should be warmed beside the fire, not heated over it. Finally it should be decanted into a pewter tankard and savoured at leisure.

The ale Simon Templar was drinking was a perfect example of that art. The Crown may be the most common pub name in England, but the inn displaying that sign in a cobbled lane under the shadow of St. Enoch's College, Cambridge, was no run-of-the-barrel beerhouse.

In summer it was almost impossible to make a path to the door through the throng of tourists. But now, with only a few days left before Christmas, the visitors were long gone and the university students who comprised the hard core of regular patrons were on vacation. Simon's only companions were a couple of ancient worthies playing dominoes, the landlord polishing glasses behind the counter, and his overfed Alsatian lying in front of the fire.

The Crown offered a choice of two bars, one small and the other tiny. Simon sat in the larger saloon, but even this measured only some twenty feet square. The ceiling was low and bowed between the rough oak beams supporting it. Pewter and brass glowed in the mellow light of oil lamps and candles. High-backed wooden settles, polished by the posteriors of countless generations of drinkers, warded off the draughts, and the blaze in the inglenook looked hungry enough to devour half a tree at one sitting. Above the mantel, poker-burned into a thick elm plank, was an exhortation to customers:

A pint in the morning to welcome the light,
A score or more between then and night.
Go to bed sober, dream without sin,
Get up in the morning and attack it agin.

Simon Templar reserved his doubts about the recommended quantity but raised his tankard to the sentiments of a simpler age.

Those whose knowledge of his life style was founded on their reading of the popular press might have been surprised to find him in such surroundings. Somehow the Crown did not fit the image of the high-living man about town which the gossip columnists projected. Nor did it reflect the picture painted by that other breed of journalist with whom he most frequently came into contact—the crime reporters. The first would not have appreciated the fact that a roaring fire, a drink, and the company of a landlord who is also a friend can be luxury enough. And as for the crime writers, they would immediately have concluded that only some illegal enterprise could have brought the Saint to Cambridge in winter. And, not for the first time in their careers of chronicling Simon Templar's actions, they would have been totally wrong. Unless, of course, there is legislation to prevent bookmakers being parted from their profits.

It had been an undramatically successful day that had begun with the impulse to leave the smog of London for an afternoon's racing at Huntingdon. It had continued with three wins in the first four races before the snow had come and caused the rest of the meeting to be abandoned. The blizzard had been so fierce that he had opted for covering the sixteen miles to Cambridge rather than the sixty-six back to town.

The storm had blown itself out by the time he had registered at one of the better hotels in the city, but the snow still lay deep and crisp and even, and the walk from the University Arms Hotel to the Crown had chilled him enough to make the mulled ale a particularly welcome form of central heating. After an hour's reminiscing with the landlord he sat beside the fire considering how to spend the remainder of the evening.

As clairvoyance was not one of the Saint's gifts, he could not know that the Angel of Adventure who so frequently and welcomingly intervened in his affairs had already made the decision for him.

The grandfather clock in the corner chimed seven, and his thoughts turned to the subject of dinner and a small restaurant off King's Parade where memory told him the food and wine would reach the standard he required. He drained his tankard and stood up. With a promise to the landlord to return the next day before starting for home, he left the inn.

The wind was still cold and sharp and he paused after

a couple of paces to pull up the collar of his sheepskin coat. One glance at the sky said there would be more snow before morning. The distant voices of carol singers drifted from the direction of St. Enoch's as he turned his back on the comforting lights of the Crown.

The lane was little more than an alley separating the confines of the college from the main thoroughfare which lay on the other side of the buildings backing onto the pub and its adjoining terrace of small shops and cottages. One hundred yards from the Crown it opened into a secluded square dominated by the tall turreted gateway of St. Enoch's.

It was a couple of years since he had last visited Cambridge, but he recalled the layout of the city well enough. The college buildings ran parallel to the river Cam with King's Parade lying on the other side of the grounds diagonally across from the square he stood in. To follow the roads round would entail a journey of more than a mile, but by cutting through the precincts the distance was nearly halved.

The gateway comprised a wide arch spanning the drive which led from the square, with two narrower tunnel-like entrances on either side for pedestrians. Heavy iron gates barred the central and right-hand openings so that visitors were channelled past the gatekeeper's rooms in the left-hand tower. Ignoring a notice stating that only those with business at the college would be admitted, the Saint strolled through and entered St. Enoch's.

The College of St. Enoch's, Cambridge, had instructed its first pupils a century before the Armada. It had been established by the rich local wool merchants eager to buy their way into the aristocracy on earth and the heaven hereafter by donating some of their gold to good works.

The elegant halls they had paid for had graced the banks of the Cam for four hundred years until progress, in the shape of nineteenth-century taste, overtook them. To the Victorian industrialists who became the college's patrons it was not enough for the seat of learning they were supporting to be old; it also had to look old. Consequently they had torn down and rebuilt or simply covered up and enlarged. The mullioned windows, the gables, and the mellow brick had disappeared beneath an avalanche of mortared flint and crude gargoyles, so that St. Enoch's had come to represent a cross between a Gothic cathedral and a romantic's idea of a medieval castle.

Although its architectural style made it appear large, St. Enoch's was in reality much smaller than many of its more famous counterparts in the city. It consisted of a rectangular central block of five storeys built around a court and flanked by two wings which looked as if they had been tacked onto either end as an afterthought. The gateway through which the Saint had just passed was set in a high brick wall which enclosed three sides of the grounds with the river forming the fourth boundary. The college stood in the middle with quadrangles to the front and sides and lawns at the rear. Each court was accessible from its neighbour via arched doorways, and there were also passages which led from the quads through the buildings to the inner court.

The courtyard he entered was paved with flagstones bordered by a gravel drive with a statue of the patron saint rising above an ornamental pond in the centre. The snow had contrived to hide the more hideous features of the façade, and its smooth whiteness gave the college an almost Dickensian Christmas-card prettiness. The court was deserted. A battered Austin saloon parked near the main steps and a solitary lighted window on the third floor were the only signs of life.

The Saint headed diagonally across the quad towards the entrance to the adjoining courtyard, which would lead him to a third, and from there to a side entrance, which he hoped would be unlocked and would deposit him within a few hundred feet of his destination. The only lighting came from a half dozen gas lamps hanging from ornate brackets fixed onto the dividing walls, but it was enough together with the whiteness of the snow and a waxing moon for him to walk briskly. As he passed the pond he heard the carol singers again, much louder this time, and guessed that they too must be using the college grounds as a short cut and keeping in practice as they went, for there could be no chance of a donation for them in the college that night.

Almost at the same instant as he heard the carollers again he saw the shadows move.

It was no more than a brief blocking of the light that filtered through the entrance to the adjoining courtyard, but it made him stop in mid-stride and the chill which crept upwards from the small of his back to the roots of his hair owed nothing to the temperature of the night. For the figure which had so fleetingly crossed his vision was that of a man clad in a flowing robe, his head and face hidden by a pointed cowl.

The Saint did not believe in ghosts, but he had seen too much in his life to disbelieve in them. Now the open mind he had always maintained on the subject was rapidly closing. The thing which had moved with such speed and silence could only have been a monk. Given that it had been the monks of the original St. Enoch's monastery who had been the recipients of the merchants' money, it was not a comforting thought.

The shock stilled him for only a moment, and then he was on his toes and racing towards the doorway. His brain registered the fact that the singing had stopped, but he gave it no conscious consideration. He reached the arch and went through without slackening speed. His eyes were automatically scanning the way ahead, searching for the mysterious figure, not looking down.

His foot caught as he cleared the shadow of the entrance and sent him pitching headlong. The loose snow sprayed around him as he hit the ground, momentarily blinding him to the cause of his fall. Instinctively he rolled away from the danger, springing upright and turning to face the man who had tripped him.

But the man made no move. He lay face down in the snow, his black overcoat only a shade darker than the shadows which had hidden him from the Saint's eyes.

The Saint knelt and carefully rolled him over while his fingers automatically felt for a pulse. But the wide staring eyes that gazed sightlessly up at him told him the search would be futile.

The body was that of a middle-aged, middle-height, middle-weight man wearing a dark business suit. A leather briefcase lay beside him but, like his pockets, appeared untouched. The length of silver twine that had killed him was still embedded deep in the flesh of his throat—flesh which despite the cold of the snow was still warm.

The realisation that the murder could only have happened seconds before made the Saint glance quickly around. But of murderers or monks there was no sign. What there was was a female of Wagnerian stature stamping hurriedly across the snow towards him. Simon held up his hand but she ignored the gesture and kept coming.

"Get the police! Hurry!" he called out, and only on the word "police" did her footsteps falter.

She stopped, stared for a few mute seconds, and then emitted a scream that would have done credit to a Valkyrie. The Saint winced, but his eyes were on the group of children clustered on the other side of the court. A few of the older, braver ones were edging nearer. He pointed towards them.

"Keep the kids away. And, for Pete's sake, shift yourself and call the police."

This time his words got through, but by then they were superfluous, for a blue uniform, attracted by the scream, was already lumbering into view.

The Saint looked from the constable to the corpse and back again. A wry smile played with the corners of his lips as he stood up. He never actually spoke the words "Here we go again." But he thought them.

2

It was three hours since he had left the Crown. Even if the clock on the interview-room wall had not told him so, his stomach would have done. The nearest the Cambridge constabulary had come to providing refreshment had been a mug of tea the colour of mahogany and the consistency of a rich soup, and a digestive biscuit so stale that a weevil would have been ashamed to be found dead in it. The beat bobby who had answered the woman's scream had summoned his superiors, and everyone had been kept waiting in the cold until the body had finally been removed and the area diligently combed for clues, of which there had appeared to be a distinct shortage. Then the Saint, the woman, and her choir of carol singers had been brought to the station and had given their statements, waited for them to be typed, and signed the same. At which point he had expected to be allowed to proceed on his lawful business of searching for sustenance.

Experience, however, had warned him that that was likely to be a forlorn hope. As soon as his identity had been established, the duty inspector had contacted his chief, and the Saint had been escorted to the interview room to await the detective's arrival. Such, at times, was the price of fame.

That detective, in the unenlightening shape of Superintendent Frederick Nutkin, now sat on the opposite side of the table, carefully reading through the Saint's statement, which he had doubtless already scanned before entering the room. If the process was intended to unsettle him it was a failure. For once the possessor of a clear conscience, Simon Templar was completely at ease, but his irritation was growing. He surveyed the detective with practised appraisal and did not like what he saw.

Superintendent Nutkin had apparently been dining out when the news reached him and had not welcomed being disturbed. Simon guessed that the celebration had been with Mrs. Nutkin. He played with the vision of a candlelit supper with a young well-proportioned blonde, but understood that a man like Superintendent Nutkin would never consider such a liaison in case it jeopardised his ambition to join the Parochial Church Council. He looked like a man whose ambition was to be a parochial church councillor: he was in his late forties, tall, wiry of frame, and sparse of hair, and exuded an aura of pomposity and pride.

Simon waited patiently for him to finish his reading. At last the superintendent laid the statement on the table between them and fixed the Saint with a suspicious stare.

"And this is everything that happened from the time you left the Crown?"

"To the last dotted *i*," the Saint said.

Nutkin scratched his chin as his eyes travelled down the typescript. Simon found the gesture annoying. Finally the detective located the passage he was looking for and read it aloud in the same dry tone he would have used for giving evidence in court.

> *"I was crossing the main courtyard and had just passed the pond when I saw a figure in the archway leading to the adjoining court. I ran towards the figure."*

Nutkin looked searchingly at the Saint.

"Why? Do you normally go chasing after everyone you see?"

"His actions appeared suspicious," Simon said blandly.

"But you say you saw this man only for a fraction of a second," Nutkin countered. "That's a very short time in which to consider him suspicious, don't you think?"

"Yes and no. Yes, I do think, and no, it isn't a short time," the Saint replied, the weariness in his voice conveying the fact that he considered the question irrelevant.

"Could it have been his clothes that made you think there was something wrong?" Nutkin asked, and the Saint showed his surprise only by the raising of a solitary eyebrow.

"The person I caught a glimpse of looked like a monk," he said evenly. "And if that sounds crazy you'll just have to believe that I'd only had two pints."

The superintendent sat back in his chair and recommenced scratching his chin.

Simon continued: "He appeared to be wearing a habit and cowl."

For a while Nutkin chewed over the information and then slowly shook his head.

"A monk, you say? Or a Father Christmas perhaps?"

Simon smiled tolerantly at the detective.

"I don't know how to tell you this, Mr. Nuthatch, but Santa Claus doesn't actually exist. Now I realise this may come as a shock but on Christmas Eve . . ."

Nutkin ignored for the moment the misrendering of his name. He waved an impatient hand, but his voice never varied its monotone.

"Very amusing. Miss Williams reports that, as she and her carol singers were entering the court where the body was found, a man dressed as Father Christmas pushed past them and ran off."

The Saint said seriously: "That would tie in. But why should someone dress themselves like that to commit murder? It seems a strange sort of disguise."

Nutkin shrugged.

"Perhaps, but effective. No one saw his face."

"Who was the dead man, anyway?"

"Sir Basil Lazentree, the Master of St. Enoch's College. He only took over at the start of the autumn term."

"I've heard of him. Doesn't he appear on one of those radio quizzes?"

"That's right," Nutkin said, and steered the interview back to the murder. "There's nothing else you can tell me?"

"Absolutely nothing, I'm afraid," said the Saint firmly. "I haven't eaten since lunch, so if you're finished with me I'd like to go."

"Yes, you can go. We'll contact you if we need you again."

The superintendent stood up and the Saint followed suit.

"We have your address in London. You'll be told when the inquest is to be opened."

"I don't think I'll be leaving Cambridge just yet, Superintendent," the Saint remarked with a smile.

Nutkin frowned.

"I can't tell you to leave the town, and I can't stop you staying," he said heavily. "But this is now a police matter, Mr. Templar. We don't need any help from you. I know your reputation, and I'm warning you not to meddle."

"Meddle, Superintendent?" said the Saint in a tone of pained surprise. "Why should I be interested in a homicidal Santa Claus who strangles people with silver twine?"

Nutkin's gaze followed the Saint down the corridor. He felt uneasy and irritable. He had often read of how Simon Templar had made the bigwigs at Scotland Yard look like so many bungling amateurs, and his official frown had masked a self-satisfied smile. It would, he had always maintained, never happen to him. The Saint's parting comments had bruised that confidence and left him strangely deflated. Suddenly it did not look like being such a happy Christmas after all.

For his part, Simon Templar hardly spared the superintendent a thought as he ate his dinner and then returned to his hotel. Nor did he wonder at the whim of the Fates who had delivered him into the hands of such an intriguing mystery; it was enough that they had. Instead, he concerned himself with the problem of where to begin looking for the murderous Mr. Claus.

Which was why, after breakfast the following morning, he entered the premises of Messrs. Drake & Humbolt. He had been directed to the small bow-windowed shop in Market Street by the hotel manager after enquiring where he might hire a costume for a fancy-dress party. Their main business came from renting out formal morning and evening wear, but he had been told that a variety of costumes were also available.

A small delicate-featured man came forward to greet him as he entered. Simon explained the purpose of his visit and the man looked doubtful.

"You're a bit late, sir, I'm afraid. Most of our customers reserve their costumes some time in advance. But we should be able to find something to suit you. What about a Roman senator or a pirate?"

"What about Father Christmas?" Simon suggested, but the assistant shook his head.

"I'm sorry, they've all gone, sir. We rent them to the department stores at the end of November, and then there are church bazaars and charity functions and so on. Regulars, you see, same people every year."

"You know most of your customers, then?"

"As I said, sir, regulars."

"Has anyone hired a Santa Claus outfit recently whom you did not know?"

The assistant looked keenly at the Saint.

"Why should you be interested in that, sir?"

"Just curious," Simon replied casually.

"The police were here this morning, sir, asking the same question. I gave them the list of customers but, as I told the officer, they were all known to us. Now, sir, about your costume."

The Saint shook his head.

"I've had another idea. Perhaps I'll cut the cost and go as Adam. Fig leaves are quite in vogue this year."

Back on the pavement he strolled idly towards St. Andrew's Street. He was not particularly disappointed. It had been the longest of long shots and he had not really expected to be told, "We had a homicidal maniac in here yesterday hiring one." But it had been worth trying.

His conversation had at least given him an idea of how to spend the rest of his morning: in the unexciting but necessary business of buying Christmas presents.

Wakeforth's was the newest and largest and unquestionably the ugliest department store in the town. Its Edwardian builders had contrived to make it look more like a four-storey mausoleum than an emporium by giving it a portico of classical dimensions and covering the façade with carvings depicting commerce throughout the Empire. But the goods displayed in the huge windows at street level were attractive enough, and inside there was at least room to move between the multitude of counters stacked with brightly packaged gifts.

The Saint browsed through the departments on the ground and first floors until he reached the second. It had been given over entirely to toys and children's clothing, and he was about to carry straight on up the stairs when a banner strung between two pillars in the centre of the floor caught his eye:

DON'T FORGET TO VISIT SANTA CLAUS
IN THE CHRISTMAS GROTTO.
A PRESENT FOR EVERYONE!

Simon grinned as he read it and decided that in the circumstances it was an invitation he could not refuse.

The Christmas grotto took up one complete corner of the floor, and consisted of a hardboard cave enclosed by cardboard cutouts of a fairy castle. The children handed their money to a bored-looking girl dressed as a pixie in a booth at the castle entrance and then walked up to where Santa sat on his sleigh in the entrance to the cave. Everything had been covered in tinsel and artificial snow and the result was obviously approved of by the line of eager children queuing at the pay booth. After their brief chat with Father Christmas the children left by a one-way turnstile at the side of the cave.

The Saint walked around the grotto and leaned against the wall beside the turnstile where he could watch the Santa at work. Close to, he looked rather less imposing than when seen from outside the grotto. Simon had no idea whether there was a regulation height for Santas but, had there been, this one would definitely not have measured up. He was little more than five feet four, and despite the bulging padding beneath his tunic quite clearly of slim build. The tunic hung loose about the shoulders and the trousers bagged at the knees. After going to so much trouble to make the grotto look attractive, it seemed strange that the management had not paid the same attention to its star attraction.

But it was not the clothes or the physique which made the Saint's eyes narrow with suspicion as he scrutinised the man. It was the face. True, the cheeks were the required rosy red, but the grease paint looked as if it had been applied with a trowel. The hood of the costume hid the forehead, and the fake cotton-wool eyebrows and luxuriant white beard contrived to conceal eighty per cent of the face. But there was no hiding the eyes, which were small and dark. He looked for final confirmation at the hands, but they were encased in thick knitted woollen gloves.

The Saint smiled thoughtfully as he nevertheless penetrated the disguise. Santa was not a he but a she.

3

The girl soon became aware that she was being watched. She pulled the hood further down over her face and shifted sideways on her sleigh so that as much of her as possible was hidden from him. Using her body to mask the gesture, she waved to the pixie in the pay booth. It was obviously a prearranged signal, for the assistant immediately closed the gate leading to the grotto and hung a notice on it promising that Father Christmas would return in thirty minutes. Santa jumped nimbly from the sleigh and with the pixie hurried towards a door marked "Staff Only."

The Saint skirted the grotto wall and followed. He was just in time to see the pixie disappearing into the lavatory a few yards along the corridor, while Santa darted through a door marked REST ROOM directly opposite.

Simon paused for a moment to be sure that the corridor was not about to be used by other members of the staff, who might be curious as to his presence, before he opened the rest-room door.

The girl was standing in the middle of the room. She had pulled off the false beard and eyebrows. She still wore the boots and red breeches, but the fur-trimmed tunic had been discarded and thrown across a chair on which also rested the cushion she had used to pad out her figure to the required traditional plumpness.

He smiled with open approval.

"Darling," he murmured, "you can come down my chimney any night of the year."

She was young, trim, and beautiful, small-featured under the now ridiculous ruddy make-up. Straight black hair slid past slender shoulders. Her eyes transmitted that combination of mystery and innocence which is the birthright of so many Eastern women.

She snatched up the tunic and clutched it modestly to her chest.

"Go away, please," she blustered indignantly. "I have to change."

"Carry on," he said coolly. "I won't watch."

He made a play of turning and closing the door and studiously averting his gaze to give her time to pull on a sweater snug enough to emphasise the charms he had already glimpsed. He read the fire regulations pinned to the wall beside him while she exchanged the boots and breeches for a pair of shoes and a skirt.

At last he turned and appraised the result.

"Well, it certainly beats the Father Christmas costume," he said.

She tried to hide her embarrassment by dabbing cold cream on her face and scrubbing it with tissues to remove the grease paint. The skin that it revealed was the colour of honey and as smooth as silk. She looked at him sullenly and spoke with a defiant edge to her voice.

"What do you want?"

The Saint perched himself on the corner of a table. It was a good question, and one to which he did not have a ready answer. He toyed with a number of possible replies before deciding on the most direct approach.

"I'm curious about why Wakeforth's employ a Miss instead of the usual Mr. Claus. Not that I'm complaining, you understand—just very interested."

She hesitated, as if she considered telling him to mind his own business, but something in his casually confident attitude told her he would not be so easily dismissed.

"If I told you, would you tell the manager?"

"I never tell on a lady," he assured her, and added: "Especially when I know her name."

His friendly tone and lighthearted manner, as much as his words, seemed to provide the reassurance she was seeking.

"My name is Chantek Alam."

"And mine is Simon Templar," he responded with a smile. "I must compliment your parents on such an apt choice of a name for you."

The Saint's knowledge of the Malay language was not comprehensive, but he remembered enough from early adventures to know that *Chantek* means "beautiful."

For the first time her tenseness began to dissolve.

"Thank you."

"Now, do I get my explanation?"

"I am a student at St. Enoch's from Singapore and I am working here during the holiday. That is all."

St. Enoch's was unique in Cambridge in those days for admitting both male and female students.

"But not as Father Christmas," said the Saint.

Chantek shook her head.

"No, as an assistant in the doll department."

At that moment a rasping snore reverberated through the air. Chantek walked across and pulled aside a curtain which cut off one corner of the room, to reveal a day bed on which was curled the slumbering form of a portly white-haired gentleman of pensionable age. His suit was crumpled and stained, the collar had come adrift from his shirt, and his face had not seen soap, water, or razor for at least twenty-four hours. The atmosphere surrounding him smelt like the discharge from a brewhouse chimney.

"That specimen is, I presume, the authentic Mr. Claus," said the Saint.

Chantek sighed as she regarded the sleeping man.

"Yes. His name is Ted, and he is really quite sweet. But sometimes he has a little too much to drink."

Simon glanced at his watch and laughed.

"At eleven in the morning?"

"Oh no," Chantek explained. "He did not feel well when he arrived this morning. I think he had been to a party last night."

"It must have been some fling. So you told him to sleep it off and you took his place?"

She nodded.

"Yes. You see, if he had tried to work in that state they would have sacked him. Mary and I—she's the pixie—just wanted to help him. He's a nice old man really, and he needs the money."

Another snore sounded from the sleeping Santa and the girl looked at him in dismay.

"I thought he would have woken up by now."

"I think we can do something to bring him back to the land of the living," Simon assured her with a grin.

One end of the rest room had been made into a kitchenette by the addition of a sink, a work surface, a few cupboards, and an electric hot plate. He removed the kettle from the ring, poured away the hot water, and replaced it with cold. Positioning it directly above the man's head, he tilted it through ninety degrees.

Ted-the-Santa's eyes opened as soon as the stream of icy water hit his brow and cascaded down his face. He coughed and spluttered, and with a convulsive heave managed to sit up. Simon continued the shower until the power of speech returned.

"'Ere, what the hell's going on?" the man demanded aggrievedly, wiping the water from his eyes as he looked from Chantek to the Saint.

Simon surveyed him coldly.

"You're going on." He consulted his watch. "In about ten minutes, if we can make you look like something resembling the kiddies' favourite and not a reject from a doss house."

The man jumped angrily to his feet as the words penetrated the congeners numbing his senses. It was not a wise move. His face twisted in pain and he collapsed back onto the day bed and sat holding his head in his hands.

"Me brain's breaking up," he whined, but the Saint had no pity.

"Chantek, brew some coffee," he said as he hoisted the man back to a vertical position and shoved him towards the sink. "And as for you, start cleaning yourself up."

The man scowled at him but slowly set about doing as he was told. Chantek put the kettle on the hot plate. She turned back to the Saint and opened her mouth to speak, but no words came out.

Simon followed her eyes and glanced over his shoulder. Framed in the doorway, staring at the scene with undisguised disapproval, stood two men.

"What is going on here?"

It was the larger of the pair who spoke, and the way the other man followed him into the room stamped them immediately as employer and employee.

Both Chantek and the drunk stood as if frozen and were obviously too stunned or too nervous to answer. As an outsider the Saint had no such inhibitions, and for no logical reason other than that he did not like his attitude or his appearance he took an immediate dislike to the man who had spoken.

He smiled benignly.

"We're rehearsing the firm's panto," he said agreeably. "I'm Prince Charming, Chantek is Cinderella, this specimen is Buttons—or will be when we've done him up. If you'd like a part, we still have to cast the Ugly Sisters."

The bigger man's cheeks burned and he appeared to be about to have a seizure. He wore a pin-striped three-piece which, despite the quality of its tailoring, could not hide a spreading paunch which was the result of too many dinners and an equally expansive rear that was the legacy of spending too much time sitting in a chair telling other people what to do.

"Who the devil are you?" he spluttered, and the Saint's smile broadened.

"Not a devil, a saint. My name is Templar. And who are you?"

The thin, lanky, and extremely ill-at-ease individual who stood at the big man's right hand answered. His tone conveyed as much surprise at the Saint's ignorance as if someone at a Buckingham Palace garden party had asked him to identify the Queen.

"This is Mr. Wakeforth. Mr. Stanton Wakeforth."

The Saint considered the revelation and appeared duly impressed.

"Not *the* Mr. Stanton Wakeforth?"

The lanky man continued to look surprised.

"Of course."

The Saint slowly shook his head.

"Sorry, I never heard of him."

It was, in fact, an outright lie but the Saint could never resist the chance to prick the balloon of pomposity whenever it blew across his path. Mr. Stanton Wakeforth, he knew from his reading of the daily papers, was founder and autocratic ruler of the chain of department stores which bore his name. Mr. Stanton Wakeforth was very rich. Mr. Stanton Wakeforth was a self-made man, and Mr. Stanton Wakeforth's greatest pleasure in life was telling people so.

The said Mr. Stanton Wakeforth glared at him.

"Are you an employee of this organisation?"

"No, sir, he isn't," answered his companion, with the look of a man who wishes he had died thirty seconds previously.

"Well, I don't know why you are here and I don't care." Wakeforth's voice trembled with barely suppressed rage. "This is a staff-only area and unless you leave immediately I'll have Security throw you out."

Before the Saint could say anything, Wakeforth turned on the others: "I heard everything you said from the corridor. I will not tolerate such behaviour in my stores. Collect your cards and get out. You are both dismissed."

Simon looked steadily at the store boss and resisted a strong urge to make his fat lips even fatter. He had been presented with a virtual invitation to deflate the man's ego and he had accepted it heartily without first considering where his action might lead. Now he felt sorry—not for what he had done, but for the consequences for Chantek and the elderly Santa. He accepted the responsibility of trying to repair the damage he had unintentionally caused.

"Look, Mr. Wakeforth, you're absolutely right, I shouldn't be here and I'll go," he said. "But there's no cause to lay the heavy hand on these two, especially Chantek. After all, she was only trying to help. Where would you have been this morning without a Santa Claus? And as for Ted here, surely everyone is permitted one lapse, especially at this festive season."

But his pleas were useless. His first impudence had infuriated the magnate beyond the point where he might have listened to rational argument.

Wakeforth turned on him savagely.

"How dare you try and tell me how to run my business, young man! Just get out of here now, all three of you."

The loudspeaker on the wall above the door crackled:

"Calling Mr. Wakeforth. Please contact your office. Mr. Wakeforth, please."

Wakeforth glared at the intercom as if he wished it possessed a neck he could wring. He grabbed the transceiver from the internal phone on the wall, dialled a couple of numbers, and bellowed his name into the mouthpiece.

His face went a shade darker as he listened.

"The stock room? Why?"

The answer clearly did nothing to ease his temper. He

banged the handset back into its cradle and addressed his aide.

"Apparently there's some flap on. Stock control want me down there straight away, personally." He wagged an accusing finger under the man's nose. "I tell you, Parsons, I don't like the way this store is being run. I don't like it at all."

Parsons blanched.

"Shall I come to the stock room with you, sir?" he suggested timorously, and only just managed to conceal his relief when the offer was refused.

"No, I'll deal with it. Though God knows why I should have to. You just get these people out of my store before I return. I'll talk to you later."

An uneasy silence followed the slamming of the door behind Mr. Stanton Wakeforth. Parsons looked apologetically at Chantek and the now abruptly sobered Santa.

"You had better come to my office straight away. I'll make your money up to the end of the week. I'm sorry, but that's the best I can do."

Simon attempted a final appeal.

"Couldn't you get him to reconsider?" he asked hopefully. "Perhaps when he's cooled down a bit."

Parsons sighed, and his regret seemed genuine.

"There is no chance of that, I'm afraid. Mr. Wakeforth doesn't cool down. He's always like that, and this has been one of those days when nothing has been right for him. I have to do what he tells me. Would you come this way, please?"

He led the dispirited trio out of the rest room, and they filed without speaking up to his office on the top floor and waited while he contacted the accounts department and arranged for the cards and wages to be sent up.

"*Tida apa,*" the Saint said to Chantek consolingly. "There must be plenty of other jobs going at this time of year. And if I can't find 'em for you, I'll have you both myself, as my personal Santas. I always wanted to feel like the Man Who Has Everything."

Her eyes had sparkled with happy surprise at the first phrase he used.

"First, you will have to tell me how you learned to speak Malay."

"It's a long story," said the Saint wickedly, "and may involve several evenings."

Parsons sat behind his desk gazing awkwardly into space. The man called Ted sat, head down, staring at the carpet. Chantek stood looking out of the window over the snow-brushed rooftops. The Saint eyed the safe in the corner and considered whether the almighty Mr. Stanton Wakeforth should be taught a lesson where it would hurt him most—in his pocket.

All four stopped their meditations as a commotion erupted in the outer office, and turned as the door was thrown back and a man in brown overalls staggered in.

"Murder!" he panted. "He's dead. I saw it!"

"What on earth are you blabbering about?" the manager demanded.

"I tell you, I saw it," the porter repeated.

"Who's been murdered?" Parsons asked sharply. "You're not making sense, man."

The porter shook himself as he fought to control his shock and regain his breath.

"Mr. Wakeforth, sir. He's been shot. Murdered! I saw it."

"Where?" The Saint's voice sliced through the stillness that followed.

The porter swung around and noticed him for the first time.

"In the stock room. Just now. I saw it!"

"Good, then you can show me. Come along."

Simon grasped the man by the arm and hustled him back to the door. He turned to the manager as he reached it. "Don't sit there gawping, phone the police."

In the corridor the porter suddenly stopped and began to struggle against the Saint's grip.

"I'm not going back down there!"

"Yes, you are," Simon told him firmly. "Don't worry, I'll hold your hand. Pull yourself together. Where is the stock room?"

The authority in his voice was not to be denied, and the porter stopped resisting and managed to get a hold on himself.

"Ground floor at the rear. I ran up the stairs, but there's a service lift."

The elevator was at the end of the passage, and Simon hustled the porter to it and bundled him inside.

The iron cage descended with infuriating slowness. The lower they went, the more the porter's agitation increased, and when they finally stopped he pressed himself into a corner and refused to budge. The Saint let him stay where he was.

There was no need to search for the body. Stanton Wakeforth lay spread-eagled on the floor a few feet from the lift. There was a neat round hole in the breast pocket of his jacket where the bullet had entered, and a crimson stain that oozed and spread from beneath him.

The Saint knelt beside the body, and his experienced eye told him all he needed to know. The scorch marks around the wound showed that the gun had been fired at point-blank range, and death had come so quickly that the magnate's features still seemed to be contorted in anger rather than fear.

Clutched in the left hand was a scrap of paper, and Simon had to open the fingers to extract it. At first he thought it was gift-wrapping paper, and then its real purpose dawned. It was part of a Christmas cracker.

The stock room covered a large area, and nearly all of it was stacked to the ceiling with crates and boxes. On one side was an open loading bay leading to a service road which ran behind the store. The Saint knew it was no use now to hunt for the murderer. It must have been simple for him to get in and hide among the crates until Wakeforth arrived, and just as easy to get away again afterwards without being seen.

He walked back to the lift and pressed the top-floor button.

"Tell me what happened," he said to the porter as the lift slowly rose.

"I was checking the inventory of the last delivery when I see Mr. Wakeforth come out of the lift. Then this figure steps out in front of him and holds out a cracker. Mr. Wakeforth tries to pull it away from him, and then there's a bang and he's dead. Shot!"

"What did this man look like?"

The porter could not stop trembling. His fingers dug into the Saint's shoulder, and his voice was little above a croak.

"I told you, I saw it. It wasn't a man. It was Father Christmas!"

4

What the *Chronicle's* front-page headline lacked in syntax it made up for in dramatic effect.

SANTA KILLER STRIKES AGAIN!

Simon Templar propped the paper against the coffeepot and read the story during breakfast.

The killing of Sir Basil Lazentree had happened too late for the following morning's papers, but the murder of Stanton Wakeforth could not have been better timed if the editor had committed it himself.

Two murders within twenty-four hours and half a mile of each other, both of important people, both killed by a man disguised as Father Christmas, and both with Simon Templar in the vicinity: the story had everything any news-hungry editor ever dreamt of.

There was an account of each murder plus potted biographies of both victims. Everyone but the cat appeared to have been interviewed, and there was a spread of pictures of every person and place in any way involved.

The Saint reviewed his own notices critically. For once the quotes were accurate, but he thought it was time the press took a new portrait for their files. The picture of Nutkin, however, was an accurate likeness, the photographer having managed to catch him looking both arrogant and angry as he shouldered his way through the throng of reporters outside the department store.

There are certain moments which transcend description, when words become not only superfluous but positively obstructive to a clear understanding of the emotions they seek to describe. The look on Superintendent Nutkin's face when he marched importantly into the manager's office and found himself confronted by the Saint had been one such moment. It was like the expression of a monarch who, after walking grandly up the aisle to be crowned, finds someone already sitting on his throne.

"What are you doing here?" he almost shouted.

"Waiting for you, like everybody else, Mr. Nuthatch—"

"Nutkin!"

"—and before you go out on a limb and I have to saw it off," Simon continued kindly, "we were all here together while Brother Wakeforth was being promoted to the Great Board Room in the sky. So let me warn you that anything you say may be taken down and used in evidence of probable paranoia."

Once he had recovered from the shock and reluctantly accepted that the Saint's alibi was not merely cast iron but made of titanium alloy, Nutkin had instituted the ritual known as Standard Procedure. The store had been cleared of customers and searched, the staff had been questioned and their statements taken, the stock room had been dusted for fingerprints and the body examined, photographed, and finally despatched to the morgue.

The net result of so much activity had been to establish that the murder of the store boss was in some way connected with the killing of the master of St. Enoch's—a fact that had been fairly obvious from the moment the porter had given his description of the murder.

A clue that confirmed a probable link between the killings had been spotted by the Saint. Left to his own devices after being clearly exonerated of Wakeforth's murder, he had ignored Nutkin's instruction to leave the store and instead wandered up to the tycoon's office. Browsing through his diary, he had found an entry: "*Lazentree 3.30.*" The date was December 23, two days away. It was unexplained. He had bought Wakeforth's secretary, who always accompanied her boss on visits to his stores, a calming brandy in a nearby pub, and she had identified the handwriting as his but had had no idea what the meeting was to have been about. Nutkin's investigation did not seem to have noted it, but it had made the Saint somewhat curious about the connection of Stanton Wakeforth with St. Enoch's.

One good thing to have resulted from Wakeforth's death was that his last ukase had been forgotten, and Chantek and Ted had been allowed to go back to their jobs. The Saint was no longer concerned with the hungover Santa, but Chantek was a different matter and had provided a delightful companion at dinner that night. Not yet having been thoroughly contaminated by the rising Western tide of feminine assertiveness, she happily and shamelessly deployed all the complaisant wiles which were the natural legacy of her other-worldly upbringing.

Simon Templar was not numbered among the ranks of those who believe that early rising leads to health, wealth, and wisdom, and he was the last customer left in the restaurant when he was finally thinking of leaving the breakfast table and officially acknowledging that the day had begun. At that moment what is commonly termed a discreet cough sounded in close proximity.

"I should take something for that," he murmured without looking up from the article he was finishing.

There was a brief pause before the intruder spoke.

"Are you Mr. Simon Templar?"

There was an officious undertone to the voice which matched the abruptness of the cough. The Saint folded his paper and eyed the newcomer speculatively.

"That depends on whether you are (a) from the Inland Revenue, (b) from a news agency, (c) from the police, or (d) looking for a donation," he replied.

On reflection, the other could not have been any of those alternatives, except just possibly the first. His pin-striped suit was too severely cut to belong to a reporter, and at around five feet seven he was a shade too small for the constabulary. There was a sharpness about the eyes and a tightness about the lips which did not suit the image of a charity worker. But rather than a tax collector he reminded the Saint of a bank manager.

The man smiled, or, to be precise, his lips twitched in what was an effort to produce a smile.

"I am Godfrey Nyall, bursar of St. Enoch's College," he stated formally. "I wonder if I might have a word with you."

Simon gestured towards the vacant chair beside him.

"Wonder no more. Sit down and have as many words as you wish. Would you like some coffee?"

Nyall accepted the chair but declined the coffee. He came immediately to the reason for his visit.

"I read in the paper this morning that it was you who found Sir Basil's body."

"That's right."

"And you were also present when Mr. Wakeforth was murdered."

"Just a knack, really," smiled the Saint, with a dismissive shrug of his shoulders.

Having established his facts, Nyall appeared uncertain how to continue, and Simon had to prompt him.

"What can I do for you?"

"I, that is, we—the senior members of the faculty—would like to talk to you. Naturally we have already spoken with the police, but with a person such as yourself involved—quite innocently of course—we thought it might be . . ."

Nyall floundered, and again the Saint came to the rescue.

"Useful? Advantageous?" he suggested.

The bursar nodded.

"Yes. It's not that we lack confidence in the police, you understand—just that a man of your reputation—that is, your experience in such matters—might be able to give us some suggestions, or—er—advice. . . ."

It was one of the most roundabout invitations Simon had received for a long time, but none the less welcome for being so. Evidently the dons of St. Enoch's had not been overimpressed with the good superintendent. And it solved the first of his problems as perfectly as if he had written the script himself.

"If there's anything I can do to help, I shall certainly be glad to do it," he said.

Nyall looked relieved.

"Thank you, Mr. Templar. Unfortunately the dean is in London today but we expect him back early this evening. Would it be convenient for you to come to the college at half past eight tonight?"

"Fine by me," Simon agreed.

He had been prepared to go with the bursar immediately but was not sorry about the delay. He had had his own plans for the day which had nothing to do with solving crime but everything to do with developing his acquaintance with Chantek, whose day off it happened to be.

The bursar took his leave, and the Saint ushered him out of the breakfast room into the hotel lobby, but after one glance at the crowd of reporters gathered between the reception desk and the door turned on his heel and eventually made a less hazardous exit via the kitchens.

A slow thaw had started and the city streets had been reduced to dirty grey strips of slush, but the flat lands of the Cambridgeshire countryside were still carpeted in white with a thin mist blurring the edges of the fields. The Saint allowed the Hirondel to idle along winding lanes, letting the starkness of the scenery be warmed by the vivacity of the girl beside him. They lunched at Newmarket and motored back in a wide loop via Bury St. Edmunds and Haverhill at a speed lazy enough to bring them back to Chantek's digs in a house near the college soon after dark, where she insisted that he come in for tea. It was cosy by the small coal fire, and when she offered to fix a snack it was difficult to remind himself that sometimes business had to be put before pleasure. But her good night was long and lingering enough to force him to hurry the last few yards to be on time at St. Enoch's for his appointment.

Godfrey Nyall collected him from the gatekeeper's lodge and led him into the central block of the college and through a labyrinth of corridors to the senior common room. It was spacious and elegant with oak-panelled walls, a deep-pile carpet, and rows of bookshelves holding richly bound volumes. The overall effect was more reminiscent of the smoking room in a St. James's club than a staff room in a university.

Two men rose to greet them as they entered, and Nyall performed the introductions.

"Professor Edwin Darslow. Professor Denzil Rosco."

The Saint shook hands and let himself be planted in a wing armchair at the hearthside. He accepted the whisky they offered, and took advantage of the pause while it was poured to observe his hosts.

Edwin Darslow looked to be about fifty, but he had that type of timeless face which is hard to date accurately. His hair was white but plentiful, and the lines that etched his features were more the furrows of concentration than the mark of passing years. He was thin to the point of gauntness, and his movements were jerky and hesitant. He perched rather than sat on his chair, and his eyes darted continually around the room as if he constantly expected to be surprised.

Denzil Rosco was a complete contrast. Dressed in comfortably rumpled slacks and a leather-patched tweed jacket, he lounged in his chair and seemed to regard both his colleagues and the Saint with a detached air of vague amusement. He was the youngest of the St. Enoch's trio, probably in his thirties, and from his build and the slight misalignment of his nose it seemed likely that he had not long ago hung up his rugby shirt for the last time.

Nyall handed round the drinks and then sat in the chair facing the Saint.

"Professor Burridge, the dean, has been delayed, I'm afraid, but he should be here shortly," Nyall informed him.

"Well, Mr. Templar, what do you make of it all?" asked Rosco with a smile. "How long before we catch this slaying Santa?"

Simon returned the grin. There was something immediately likeable about the man, perhaps because he appeared less dusty and formal than his colleagues.

"I don't make anything of it—yet. And I haven't got the faintest idea how long it will take to catch him," Simon said truthfully.

Nyall looked slightly offended by the Saint's bluntness. "You mean they may never catch this madman?"

The Saint shook his head.

"Oh, he'll probably get caught sometime, if he makes a mistake, and most murderers eventually do. But I wouldn't dismiss him as a madman if I were you. He may be obsessed, he may even be slightly deranged, but he's sane enough to know exactly what he's doing and plan it well beforehand."

"How do you mean, exactly?" Nyall asked.

"Madmen don't time their murders so well. He knew when Sir Basil would be alone and where. He knew Wakeforth was visiting his Cambridge store, he knew how to get into the loading bay, use the internal telephone to contact him, and what excuse to use to put him on the spot. Not only that, he's intelligent and cunning enough to work out a brilliant disguise. A Santa Claus costume is a practically total cover-up, and yet at this time of year it doesn't arouse any suspicion. He could use it again and still get away with it, because nobody would expect him to make himself so conspicuous."

"Do you think he will kill again?" Darslow asked.

"There's an old superstition that things always go in threes."

"So we just hang around until he decides to kill somebody else and hope he leaves a footprint or a cigarette butt or a trail of blood or some such clue so that the worthy Superintendent Nutkin can do his Sherlock Holmes act," Rosco said cheerfully.

"We're really interested to know—as, er, off-the-record fans of yours—what you'd be doing in the meantime, if you were in Nutkin's place," said Nyall.

"I'd be looking for a motive," said the Saint, "and hoping that it would point me to a suspect. You knew Sir Basil, have you any idea why somebody should want to murder him?"

He looked at each of the three men in turn as he spoke. Both Nyall and Rosco returned his gaze negatively, but Darslow concentrated on the liquid in his glass and avoided a direct encounter. His nervousness was so apparent that the Saint warned himself against jumping to conclusions.

But before any of the three dons could answer his question, the door opened to admit a tall imperious individual who could only be the dean. A pace behind him trailed the less imposing figure of Superintendent Nutkin.

"Why, here's the man himself!" Simon exclaimed joyfully. "How've you been getting on with your enquiries, Mr. Nutcase?"

The look on the detective's face when he saw the Saint suggested a sudden violent attack of indigestion.

"What are you doing here, Templar?" he demanded in a strangled voice which indicated that his pains were getting worse.

"Nothing much, just passing the evening trying to solve a couple of homicides," the Saint said breezily. "And you? Have you come to enrol for a degree in detection or did you just slip in before they shut the door?"

The dean, whose gaze had flittered between the two

like an umpire at a tennis match, stepped into the breach of the peace.

"I ran into the superintendent on my way from the railway station," he explained. "I thought it might be helpful if he joined us for an informal chat. I presume that you are Mr. Simon Templar. I am Dr. Burridge, the dean of St. Enoch's."

Burridge's solemn monotone matched his sombre features. His handshake was strong and authoritative. Nutkin tried to ignore the Saint with the same dedication he might have used to try to forget an aching tooth. When he and the dean were seated, Nyall summarised the conversation they had missed, up to the Saint's question.

"Can any of you gentlemen think of anyone who might have had a grudge against Sir Basil?"

Burridge slowly shook his head.

"You must remember, Mr. Templar, that Sir Basil had only been Master here for a few months. I don't think any of us knew him before then, although naturally we knew *of* him because of his broadcasting activities. As far as I know, he made no enemies since he came here."

Denzil Rosco's mouth curved in a cynical smile.

"Only the spiders," he drawled, with a mischievous sidelong glance at the bursar.

"I beg your pardon?" said Nutkin sharply.

"I meant that only spiders might take a dislike to people who brush away cobwebs."

"What Professor Rosco may be trying to say," Nyall explained, "is that some of us did not like a few of Sir Basil's ideas for the future of the college."

"And what where they?"

"Oh, nothing much," Rosco said lightly. "He just wanted to bring St. Enoch's into the twentieth century."

"St. Enoch's is not as old or as famous or as rich as many of the Cambridge colleges," Nyall said starchily, sitting forward in his chair and glaring at Rosco. "But that doesn't mean that we do not have our traditions and that we are not proud of them."

"But you still haven't told us what his plans were," the Saint reminded them.

Again it was the dean who intervened like the chairman of an unruly committee. He spoke quickly to prevent either Nyall or Rosco from continuing their apparent feud.

"That is because we do not know. Sir Basil talked in generalisations—about getting new patrons to endow new fellowships in new and perhaps controversial subjects. He had not taken us into his confidence about anything specific. It was mainly his general attitude that may have struck some of us as a bit commercial and unacademic."

"But not upset them enough to make anyone think of murdering him, I suppose?" Nutkin asked.

Edwin Darslow gave a short nervous laugh. It was the first sound he had made for such a long time that it drew all eyes to him. He shifted uncomfortably in his chair as he realised he had become the focus of attention.

"I hardly think anyone would take us for murderous types, Superintendent," he said hastily, in a voice a tone higher than it should have been.

"You'd be surprised," Nutkin said rather smugly, "if you met some of the murderers I've had to deal with."

"All caught with your own bare hands?" said the Saint with mock admiration.

The summons of the telephone splintered the tension that was building again.

Nyall lifted the receiver and then handed it to Nutkin.

The superintendent listened for a few moments, his expression indicating that his indigestion had returned with a vengeance.

"All right," he said. "I'll be there in five minutes."

He dropped the receiver into its cradle and faced the gathering.

"I'm sorry, gentlemen," he said heavily, "but I have to return to the station immediately."

"Another murder?" asked the Saint hopefully.

"I have to brief the chief constable on the progress of our enquiries," Nutkin said, with a return to his usual pompous manner. But there was something about it which suggested that he would have preferred being summoned to deal with a dead body rather than a live one with gold braid on its shoulders.

The dons rose as the detective made to leave. Their eagerness for the amateur-Sherlock session had clearly evaporated, and the Saint realised that little was likely to be gained by pressing the subject at that moment. He contented himself with the thought that he could always come again.

The goodbyes were brief, and a few minutes later the Saint found himself walking across the main courtyard beside Nutkin. The detective did not seem to welcome his company and Simon saw no reason to force a conversation from which he would learn exactly nothing. Nutkin's car was parked in the square, and the Saint lingered beneath the main gateway and watched him drive away.

He leaned against the wall while his gaze roamed round the quadrangle. Except for the quantity of snow it was identical to when he had cut across it and discovered Lazentree's body. But though everything seemed to be the same he had a nagging feeling that it was in some way different.

As he stood scanning the scene and trying to decipher the subtle change that had taken place, a lone figure hurried down the college steps and headed for the doorway into the adjoining court with a large package under his arm.

"A bit early for delivering Christmas presents," the Saint observed to himself thoughtfully. "Even for a Santa Claus."

Keeping close to the wall, he followed Professor Edwin Darslow into the neighbouring courtyard, past the spot where Sir Basil had been murdered, and out into a narrow close of terraced cottages that bordered the college grounds.

Staying in the protective shadows of the doorway that gave onto the pavement, he watched Darslow cross the road and stop beside a car. After a hurried glançe each way as if to assure himself that the coast was clear, the professor opened the rear hatch and put the parcel inside.

The Saint smiled softly in the darkness and blessed the impulse that had prompted him to follow the professor. Darslow's actions were curious enough by themselves, but there was something else that made his smile tighten, as he remedied the memory lapse that had worried him a few minutes before. The car was a battered Austin saloon, and the last time he had seen it was in the main courtyard of St. Enoch's a few moments before Sir Basil Lazentree was murdered.

5

With a final furtive look around, Darslow let himself into the nearest cottage. The slamming of the door was immediately followed by the scrape of a bolt being shot home. A moment later a light came on behind the curtains of the broad downstairs window.

The roadway and pavement were deserted, but lights showed in several other windows on the street. Simon lingered in the shadows until he was sure that neither the professor nor his neighbours were looking out from behind their curtains. Satisfied that he would be unobserved, he crossed the road and tried the handle at the blunt end of the Austin. It was securely locked. Had he been carrying even the most rudimentary instrument, the mechanism would not have survived his probing for more than a few seconds, but he had not expected for a moment to need any such thing when he set out.

He straightened quickly and glanced along the close at the sound of a door opening and the clatter of milk bottles on the step. Conscious of how suspicious he looked, he turned on his heel and walked briskly back to the college gate from where he could see Darslow's cottage and most of the close without being visible himself.

Analysed individually, the three pointers that came together to make Professor Edwin Darslow a suspect were each completely innocuous. Why shouldn't his car be parked outside the college wherein he worked? Why shouldn't he put a parcel in the boot of the aforementioned automobile? And why shouldn't an academic who has spent his life surrounded by books be ill at ease in the company of the most notorious outlaw of his generation, especially when the said outlaw is investigating the murder of the said academic's boss? The Saint was fully aware that he might be adding one and one and one and making four. But it was the only equation that had so far presented itself, and he wasn't going to dismiss it until he had double-checked the arithmetic.

Short of hammering on Darslow's door, dragging him out, and forcing him to open his car and the mysterious package, which would have lacked a certain degree of subtlety, there were only two options open. One was to return to the hotel and bring back the kit of burglarious implements which he always carried with him in readiness for all contingencies; the other was to do nothing and wait on events.

While the Saint considered the alternatives the light downstairs was extinguished and after a few moments another came on in the room above. Ten minutes later that too went out.

His watch showed ten forty-five, which seemed a fairly early bedtime unless the professor was planning an equally early start in the morning. The Saint waited for a further five minutes, to assure himself that Darslow had done nothing more exciting than go to bed, before retracing his steps through the college grounds and heading back for his hotel. Whatever Edwin Darslow's plans for the following day, it seemed an odds-on chance that they included the parcel and its contents. Simon decided that it might prove more interesting to keep an eye on the professor and his package than to pre-empt events by breaking into the car.

In spite of Simon Templar's scepticism about the virtues of early rising, there were occasions when his vocation made such tiresome activities mandatory. The sun rose at seven twenty-five the next morning and the Saint witnessed its first rays pierce the sky from behind the wheel of the Hirondel. Faced with the choice of enduring the discomforts of keeping the house and its occupant under surveillance all night or of returning early in the morning and risking missing Darslow's exit, he had gambled on the latter. The fact that the professor's car was still in the same spot, and he had arrived in time to see the bedroom light switched on, showed that the bet had paid off.

He had parked the Hirondel at the T junction where the close met a quiet side road which in turn connected with the main thoroughfares of the city. Through the side window he could see the entire close at a glance, while the windscreen provided a clear view of the road leading to the city centre, the direction in which anyone leaving the close was most likely to go.

He leaned across and pushed open the passenger door in response to a rap on the window. Chantek slid into the seat beside him.

She smiled brightly.

"Good morning."

Simon looked at her doubtfully.

"Is it? I've been here an hour and he hasn't done anything more exciting than take in the milk."

Chantek delved into the carrier bag she had brought and produced a vacuum flask and a stack of bacon sandwiches.

"Coffee?"

"That's the best offer I've had today," he said gratefully.

Aware that he would have to leave the hotel before the

kitchen started serving breakfast, he had taken the precaution of calling Chantek the night before and enlisting her help in combating early morning hypoglycemia, though he was not entirely motivated by the need for nutrition. The department store was closed out of respect, and he had his own ideas about how to fill the time on her hands.

He turned in his seat to take the mug from her and grimaced at the stiffness of his joints.

"I've just made medical history. I'm the first person to get rigor mortis while still breathing," he complained.

Chantek was not sympathetic.

"It serves you right for suspecting Professor Darslow. He looks such a timid little man."

The Saint sipped the hot brown liquid and sighed at the rapid thaw it produced in his arteries.

"So did Crippen and Christie," he pointed out.

"I still don't believe it," Chantek said firmly.

The Saint nodded towards the cottage as he saw its front door opening.

"Well, we shall see. It looks as though we're going into business at last."

Chantek followed his eyes and watched Darslow leave the cottage and get into his car.

The Saint put a hand on her shoulder and drew her down beside him below the level of the dashboard as the Austin chugged past them heading for the centre of town. The rakish lines of the Hirondel would have drawn curious attention in Piccadilly; in that staid and sleepy backwater the cream and red speedster was as much in harmony with its surroundings as a tuba in a string quartet. For once he wished he had been driving something more sedate, but as he had not used it to go to the college there was no reason why anyone seeing it should associate it with him: it could as well have belonged to some very well-heeled undergraduate. At any rate, it did not seem to affect Professor Darslow's progress.

Cautiously Simon peeped over the rim of the steering wheel and noted that the professor had not bothered to scrape the overnight frost from the rear window. Until the sun or the car's heater dissolved the grey crystal coating, it would not be easy for him to discover that he was being followed.

The Hirondel awoke with a roar that slipped into rhythmic purring as he flicked the stick into gear and swung out on the trail of the Austin, steering with one hand and munching a bacon sandwich held in the other.

Darslow drove at a steady forty miles an hour once they had cleared the limits of Cambridge, and the Saint remained a regular fifty yards astern. As they followed the main highway towards Saffron Walden he brought the conversation back to the fellows of St. Enoch's.

"If you think Professor Edwin Darslow is far too meek and mild to be a murderer," he remarked thoughtfully, "why does he have that shifty and evasive manner?"

"I think he's terribly shy. But he's rather sweet."

It was not the objective observation he would have preferred, and Chantek, sensing that he was hoping for something more substantial, continued: "It doesn't seem likely that someone who lectures in law would commit a crime."

The Saint smiled to himself as he thought of all the pillars of propriety he had known, from Cabinet ministers and judges to a few police officers, who were always lecturing in law in one way or another but had not always been known to practise their teachings themselves. But he let the matter rest and went on to see if he could learn any more about Darslow's colleagues.

"What do you know about Professor Rosco?" he asked.

"He's sweet."

"Are all professors sugar-coated as far as you're concerned?" Simon enquired, half amused by her innocence and half exasperated by her vagueness.

"What I mean," Chantek explained with slow deliberation, "is that Professor Darslow is sweet like an uncle, but Rosco is *mmmmm* sweet."

The seductive purr made the Saint chuckle.

"I get the message. Is he one of your tutors?"

"No, bad luck. I'm reading English, and he lectures on zoology," she said with a sigh.

Rosco was clearly a more stimulating topic of conversation, and she needed no prompting to continue.

"He's really very clever and he has been all over the world on expeditions. Borneo, the Amazon, Africa, everywhere. When he came here last year there was a feature on him in the university magazine, full of pictures of him wading through swamps and hacking through jungles and things. Last summer he went to Kenya to study the animals in one of the national parks and almost got killed by a leopard."

"Sounds like stirring stuff," Simon agreed.

"He doesn't approve of hunting, but he had to kill it with a single shot just as it sprang," Chantek said.

The Saint, who had firsthand knowledge of the speed of a big cat going for the kill and the reflexes needed to stay alive, was duly impressed.

"He must be a good shot."

"He's won prizes for it. There's a whole cabinet full of

them in his study, and he helps to run the shooting club of the university too."

"Is that so?" he murmured, and was silent as he considered what Chantek had told him.

He had thought Rosco out of place the night before because he appeared less fusty than the others, and his global wanderings certainly provided a reason why he should be more open-minded than they. The fact that he could also handle himself in a tight corner and knew his way around a firearm was of even greater interest.

"I don't think that either Dr. Burridge or Mr. Nyall really approves of him," Chantek was saying, and he filed his thoughts for the moment and returned to the present.

"Why not?"

She shrugged.

"Oh, I don't know really. They're so stuffy and always going on about the college and its traditions, and he's not a bit like that."

She paused, and he was about to press her for more information about the college administrators when the Austin indicated right and turned off the main highway onto a secondary road. The Saint followed, and before he could restart the conversation a signpost announced that they were coming to the village of Bucksberry.

As English villages go, it was neither historically nor visually interesting, but on that particular morning it did have a certain picturesque charm owing to the riders and their pack of yapping hounds who were gathered on the green outside the aptly named Fox Inn. With the last traces of snow still clinging to the rooftops, it could have been a scene straight from a Victorian painting.

Darslow stopped in the pub's forecourt next to a group of locals who were watching the preparations for the morning's hunt. Simon tucked the Hirondel behind the cover of a conveniently placed van outside the general store on the opposite side of the road and switched off the engine.

The professor clambered out of his car and began talking to two or three of the men standing on the pavement. The Saint wound down his window but was too far away to hear what was said, and to leave the Hirondel would have risked instant recognition if Darslow looked his way. The conversation appeared, however, to consist more of arm pointing and head nodding than verbal communication.

Darslow's dress of Wellington boots, tough cord trousers, and chunky rollneck sweater beneath a heavy homespun jacket blended perfectly with the clothes of those he talked to and with the environment generally. If the rest of the day was to be spent roaming the countryside, the Saint began to fear that his Bond Street car coat and Savile Row jacket and slacks might place him at a conspicuous disadvantage.

"What's he doing, Simon?" Chantek asked.

"I'm not sure, but by the look of it he's being given directions. We'll just have to wait and see where to."

Although he could not hear Darslow's conversation there was no difficulty in hearing the remarks of the nearer riders and hunt followers as they drained their stirrup cups and speculated on the sport ahead of them. Dominating the group and clearly in charge of it was a red-jacketed rider whose heavy roan gelding stamped impatiently on the turf. The man, like his horse, was large and powerfully built. His features were strong and florid and he controlled his mount with the sureness of an accomplished horseman.

The whippers-in were ordering the hounds and the landlord of the inn was collecting the last of the stirrup cups, indicating that the hunt was about to move off. He retrieved the big red-coated rider's cup last of all and smiled diffidently at the man, who had every air of being the master of the hunt.

"Should be a good day, Colonel," he said chattily.

"Damn well hope so," the colonel muttered, and briskly caught up with his companions on the way through a gate beside the inn where they trotted out into the open fields beyond. Once through the narrow opening they fanned out and broke into a canter behind the vanguard of sniffing canine noses.

Darslow got back into his car as the pack set off and headed out of the village in the opposite direction to the way he had entered it. Simon waited until he had rounded the first bend and then pulled out in pursuit.

Bucksberry rests in a shallow scoop of land between two low tree-crested ridges. The village consists of little more than a couple of dozen houses, most of them strung out along each side of the one main street like beads on a necklace. From the back fences of the houses the fields run flat for half a mile before beginning to slope gently upwards. The road meanders for nearly a mile before forking into two lanes which curve around the base of each hill.

At this junction Darslow turned left. As he followed, the Saint glanced across the fields to his right and saw the hunters reach the end of the flat land and begin heading uphill along a path that would take them through a broad gap in the trees and over to the open country on the other side.

Darslow's next move was so unexpected that the Saint

had to brake hard to avoid coming up too close behind him. As the Austin rounded the foot of the hill it made a sudden right turn through a gateway onto a rutted cart track leading towards the top of the hill.

Simon cruised the Hirondel around the next bend, and as soon as the hedges hid them he came to a halt in a fortunate pull-off beside a farm gate.

"What do you think he's up to?" Chantek asked.

"It must be something to do with the hunt," said the Saint. "Or one of the hunters. At the pub, he must have been trying to find out where they were going to have their first try at drawing a fox. The answer must have been the woods on top of that hill, and he's meaning to get there first."

"But what for?" she persisted.

"Maybe he's one of those fox-hunting buffs who can't ride or can't afford a horse and like to follow the action on foot."

He got out of the car and watched the Austin pulling itself up the track. At the top of the hill it stopped and Darslow climbed out. He walked quickly around to the back, unlocked it, and lifted out the package he had put there the night before. The hunt was now halfway up the slope, the huntsman shouting encouragements to the hounds as they cast about for a scent.

Chantek scrambled out of the Hirondel and looked at the Saint uncertainly.

"Stay here and watch Darslow's car," he ordered, and without further explanation he vaulted over the gate and sprinted towards the spinney which the professor was entering.

He covered the quarter mile of steep gradient in a shade over sixty seconds and reached the edge of the copse before Darslow had made his way very far into it. With the skill of an Indian scout Simon dodged quickly and soundlessly between the trees until he was no more than a good stone's throw behind the professor.

Darslow tramped as quickly as the undergrowth would allow along a diagonal course that eventually brought him out on a footpath that bisected the wood and linked the fields either side of the ridge. In a moment he went behind a bush, knelt down, and seemed to be unwrapping his mysterious package.

Simon moved stealthily closer. From the corner of his eye he could see the first of the hounds enter the gap between the trees. Close on their tails came the huntsman and the whips, followed by other riders led by the colonel.

The top of the ridge formed a small plateau some two hundred yards across, and the leading riders were still only a third of the way into the wood when the crack of a single pistol shot sliced like a bullwhip through the still morning air.

Every bird in Cambridgeshire seemed to take wing at once. Their squawks and the noise of their flapping wings almost managed to cover the startled cries of the other riders and the neighing of the colonel's mount as it reared. But the colonel made no sound. He appeared to move in grotesque slow motion as his arms flew wide and he pitched backwards out of the saddle and lay still where he landed.

6

The riders who had been nearest him reined in their horses sharply, wheeling them as if instinctively forming a protective cordon around the shot man, while those who had been bringing up the rear of the hunt spurred forward to see what was happening. One of the leaders tried to wave them back as the huntsman dismounted and knelt anxiously beside the spread-eagled figure.

For a quartet of heartbeats the Saint stayed as motionless as the tree that shielded him while his brain absorbed the full import of what he had witnessed. The shot had sounded fairly close and from somewhere directly ahead. As his eyes probed the terrain to try to pinpoint its exact source, the bushes quivered and Darslow half rose from his hiding place less than a dozen yards away.

The undergrowth was denser here than in the part of the wood through which he had stalked the professor. The briers ran like hurdles between the rose-set trees, and together with the carpet of decaying leaves and twigs made moving both quickly and silently almost impossible. Simon opted for speed rather than stealth. Had Darslow been alert he could easily have heard the Saint coming but he was too preoccupied with what was happening along the path to his left.

The first the professor knew of his approach was when Simon's forearm snaked across his vision and clamped across his throat. At the same time a band of steel seemed to fasten on his right wrist as his arm was bent back and hoisted roughly along the line of his spine. The message in his ear was unchallengeable.

"One squeak and I'll break your arm. Understood?"

Darslow nodded his head the fraction that was all the freedom the Saint's hold allowed.

Simon released his grip on the other's wrist but kept the back hammer in position with the pressure of his body. With fast and expert thoroughness he ran his free hand over the professor's clothes. When the search produced no weapon he switched his attention to the ground, but the only object in view was the mysterious parcel which lay open at Darslow's feet. It did not contain a Santa Claus costume as the Saint had originally half hoped. Instead, all that spilled from the waterproof wrapping was a large bundle of rags which exhaled a malodorous mixture of aniseed and paraffin.

Along the path the riders' initial shock was beginning to wear off. Others had now dismounted and were standing or stooping uncertainly around the colonel's body. Another scarlet-coated man appeared to be taking charge. He shouted instructions in an authoritative tone that easily carried the hundred yards to where Simon and Darslow stood, detailing two members of the hunt to go for help. As they turned their horses and set off at a gallop back towards the village, he turned his attention to some braver souls who were beginning to explore the woods on either side and another who was edging cautiously along the track.

"Come back, you fools, do you want to get killed as well?" he called, and they hesitated, neither returning to the cluster around the colonel nor going farther.

The Saint sensed that their indecision was temporary. They were younger than most of their companions and looked as if they might find the gamble exciting. He and Darslow were protected by a thick screen of trees and bushes which would also hinder the horses if the riders decided to comb the wood, but if they rode along the path they would certainly be seen.

"Where's the gun?" Simon demanded softly.

"I never had one," Darslow gasped. "I only meant to sabotage the hunt. Someone else—I didn't see—"

The denial had an unmistakeable ring of truth, and Simon relaxed his throttling grip.

Events had moved quicker than the time taken to relate them and it was still barely three minutes since the sniper had fired. But the Saint grimly acknowledged that the lapse was likely to be more than long enough.

He found no fault with his own reactions. Darslow had been the obvious suspect and the Saint had tackled him without considering an alternative. He had tracked the professor diagonally across the wood and felt confident that he would have spotted anyone else hiding there. But the path split the wood in two and the other half was unexplored territory.

He dragged Darslow down so that the undergrowth screened them as much as possible, and released him.

"Go back the way you came and go fast," he whispered. "Try not to be spotted. I'll see you later at the college."

Without waiting to see if Darslow obeyed he covered the remaining few yards to the edge of the path, bent low, and then rose to sprint across the open glade. Someone shouted as the Saint reached the centre of the path, but he was moving fast with the line of his body turned away and, given the distance that separated them, he doubted that he would later be recognised. Meanwhile, that unavoidable glimpse of him would decoy any ambitious huntsman away from the direction that Darslow should have taken.

Once again hidden by the trees, he paused and looked back. The rider had made no attempt to follow up his sighting, but others who had been casting round at the sides of the path had now joined him, and the Saint guessed that their collective courage would be enough to prod them forward.

He glanced about him. This part of the wood was the same as the one he had just left, except that if anything the undergrowth was even wilder and the trees even closer together, offering the perfect cover for either a sniper or a fugitive.

He was aware of the recklessness of his actions. He was going unarmed in pursuit of a murderer who was not only packing a gun but knew how to use it, and use it well. And now his line of retreat was cut. But if Simon Templar had always bothered with such considerations there would have been very few stories to write about him.

He was about to move on when something glinting dully at his feet caught his eye. It was a spent cartridge, a .22 long rifle, and still not quite as cold as the ground when he picked it up. He slipped it into his pocket. The thick carpet of leaf mould was dented where the sniper had lain in wait. It was the perfect spot for an ambush, offering a clear view of anyone entering the wood from the direction of the village while at the same time providing the maximum amount of concealment.

Cautiously the Saint went on. With every sense alive to the movements and sounds that surrounded him, he dodged from one tree to another but saw and heard nothing except the furred and feathered inhabitants of the wood disturbed by his passing. He had gone only some three hundred yards when the trees suddenly thinned and he found himself unexpectedly at the outer edge of the wood. The ploughed fields that dipped away before him would not have offered cover to anything larger than a rabbit.

Keeping to the edge of the wood where the going was fastest, he skirted it around the top of the hill on the opposite side to the village. He went farther down the hillside as he approached the far end of the path, using the slope of the land to hide him from the riders who had ventured to the place where he had crossed.

He gained the spot where he had first entered the wood in pursuit of Darslow without further incident, and noted that the professor's car was gone as he raced down the hillside towards his own. The sooner that Bucksberry and its immediate environs were several miles astern the happier he would feel.

Chantek was still standing on the grass verge where he had left her. She opened her mouth to speak but he bundled her unceremoniously into the Hirondel and threw himself behind the wheel. In one fluid movement he gunned the engine into life. Chantek was still closing her door when the big car leapt forward like a cheetah. He hurled it along the twisting lanes and neither spoke until the first mile was covered and Chantek got her voice back.

"I saw Professor Darslow drive away. What happened?"

In clipped sentences he told her, but his mind was roving far ahead of his words.

There was no clue this time to link the killing of the colonel to the murders of Wakeforth and Lazentree, no hooded Santa or diary reminder. But his instinct told him that it was a strand of the same web. Cambridge is a peaceful city where the majority of citizens are concerned with arguments rhetorical. A third murder in three days was too much of a coincidence. There had to be a common reason not only for the killings themselves but for why they all had to occur in such quick succession and thereby make life so much more difficult for the murderer.

The Saint considered the ingredients of each killing as he searched for a connecting link that would help to build up a picture of the murderer. Lazentree had been strangled, which had required strength or a certain technique. Wakeforth's murder pointed to careful planning and a steady nerve. The shooting had called for a high degree of woodcraft and workmanship.

Chantek's comment cut through his thoughts.

"At least it proves that Professor Darslow isn't a murderer," she said with an air of triumph.

"It proves nothing except that he didn't kill the colonel," he said meticulously.

A worried frown tried to spoil the natural gayety of her features.

"Shouldn't you have stayed until the police arrived?"

The Saint chuckled at the vision the idea conjured up. "Of course I should have, but I was thinking of Superintendent Nutkin's blood pressure. If he'd found me on another murder scene, he might have had a stroke."

"But what if he finds out you were there?" Chantek persisted.

"I may even have to tell him eventually, I don't know yet. But it's unlikely that anyone could identify me. Except Darslow—and I don't think he'll be so keen to admit that he was there himself."

He did not mention the cartridge he had found, for no other reason than that it would have led to more questions which he was not ready to answer. He might have to hand it to the police at some time, but not before it had told him as much as it could without the full laboratory treatment.

Not wanting to catch up with Darslow and seem to be hounding him, he eased his throttle and took a slightly circuitous route back to Cambridge that would give the professor plenty of time to get home ahead of them.

The girl sensed his desire for silence and said little more until the Hirondel was parked outside St. Enoch's and she had directed him to Darslow's office.

"Is this the end of our day out together?" she pouted.

"I hope not, but you never know. Can I check with you in your rooms towards lunchtime?"

She nodded, and he left her with a light kiss on the cheek.

"Now let's see what Brother Darslow has to say for himself," the Saint speculated softly as he opened the professor's door.

Professor Edwin Darslow looked like a man who has aged ten years in one morning. He sat behind his desk in the small tidy confines of his study and gazed out of the window at the courtyard below without seeing anything. He still wore the country clothes he had been out in. A bottle of whisky stood on the desk blotter with a half-full tumbler beside it. As Simon entered he turned reluctantly to face him.

Simon leant against a bookcase and eyed him coldly. Darslow shifted uneasily and tried to avoid looking directly at him.

"Let's start with some explanations," said the Saint. "Like what you were doing this morning."

Darslow jerked his head.

"I told you, I wanted to sabotage the hunt," he mumbled, his cheeks tinging with embarrassment at the confession.

"Go on," Simon commanded.

Darslow's voice was hoarse and faltering as he continued.

"I don't hold with fox hunting, or any other blood sport. But a man in my position, well, I can't take part in activist demonstrations. But I thought I ought to be doing something besides talking. So I thought I'd do this on my own. I left it too late or I would have been gone before the hunt arrived. I just meant to scatter the rags around and lead the hounds astray. It's the smell of the aniseed mainly, it confuses them."

He paused and shook his head as if to clear the memories it contained.

"I had no idea what was going to happen. It was horrible, horrible. Poor Colonel Harker. Shot. It's almost unbelievable."

His voice trailed away and the Saint allowed him a few moments to pull himself together before asking: "Did you see anyone else? Anyone in the other part of the wood?"

"No, no one. I was too busy with my own work. You have to believe me, I didn't know what was going to happen."

The Saint did believe him. His distress was too real to be simulated.

"Didn't you see who it was?" Darslow asked.

"No. Our sniper was very cool. Whoever he is, he certainly knew what he was doing this morning," Simon admitted with grudging respect. "He must have hid until I passed and then doubled back, or alternatively just laid low until I'd left altogether."

"What will I tell the police?" Darslow asked.

"Nothing," Simon replied crisply. "Why bother? They don't know you were there. And if you keep quiet they probably won't find out that I was around either. Tell me what you know about this Colonel Harker, Professor."

Darslow shrugged.

"There isn't much I can tell you, Mr. Templar. He has a farm near Bucksberry and he is also head of the family building business. Quite an important man locally, and very rich too, I understand. He is—that is, was the master of the hunt. Really that's about all I know. We didn't exactly move in the same circles."

The professor paused, and his eyes kept shifting with their chronic evasiveness.

"Of course we can't be sure that he *is* dead. He might just have been wounded," he ventured.

The Saint considered the idea and dismissed it almost entirely.

"It's in the realms of possibility, but I've a feeling it's almost a certainty that our gunman was a sharpshooter, and it looked to me as if the colonel died right there in the saddle."

The word "sharpshooter" had jolted in his brain as his lips framed the syllables. For the first time since the murder of Colonel Harker he smiled.

Darslow seemed to sense the change that had come over him and glanced towards him expectantly, still without quite meeting his eyes. But if he hoped for some startling revelation, he was to be disappointed.

"I'll see you later," was all Simon said as he turned to leave.

"May I ask where you are going, if not to the police?"

The saintly smile broadened.

"To see a man about a lion," he replied helpfully.

And then he was gone.

7

Simon Templar had a way of disappearing like that when he wished to avoid explaining his actions. His exit line had been flip, but Chantek would have understood it. He felt certain that the key to everything that had happened was hidden somewhere within the college or in the brain of one of its staff. And the same intuition warned him that the events which had embroiled him had not yet completed their mysterious purpose, so the less the elders of St. Enoch's knew of his plans the more he might discover about theirs.

The porter at the entrance told him where to find a door bearing the name of Denzil Rosco. The Saint knocked, waited for a summons to enter, and, receiving none, went in anyway.

Rosco's study was a direct contrast to the room he had just left. Darslow's was tidy to the point of primness, whereas Rosco's was more of an organised shambles. It was the difference between a solicitor's office and a student's den. The law tutor's shelves had bowed beneath the weight of obese tomes bound in leather. The zoologist's bookcases were packed with large glossy-covered works and well-thumbed paperbacks, which spilled out into small stacks on the floor, on chairs, and across a table that separated two tall filing cabinets on the opposite side of the room; and what little space they left was littered with bulging files, magazines, and notebooks.

On one side of the door was a large map of the world dotted with different-coloured flags so that it resembled a global golfcourse, but there was no clue to what they indicated. Taking up most of the space on the other side was a display cabinet mounted on a low three-drawer chest, which contained the trophies Chantek had mentioned.

They made an impressive collection, illustrating in silver and bronze their owner's skill with rifle, shotgun, and, most interestingly, pistol. Lined above the chest were framed photographs of Rosco in various exotic landscapes.

His desk backed onto a high bay window that looked across the east quadrangle directly in line with the spot where Sir Basil Lazentree had been murdered. The Saint sat at the desk and routinely tried the drawers. All were unlocked, but each contained only the miscellaneous stationery that could be expected.

The display cabinet faced the desk, and his attention returned to the array of cups and salvers. Rosco's marksmanship was, after all, the prime object of his interest.

He rose and crossed the room and opened each drawer in turn. The contents of the first two drawers were unexciting. A telescopic sight in its case, a ramrod, rags and oil for cleaning a rifle, a shoulder sling for carrying same, a cartridge belt minus cartridges, some small paper targets whose groupings of holes testified to the prowess of the man who made them, a canvas pouch of indeterminable use, a pair of binoculars, and some back copies of *Shoot-*

ing Monthly. The bottom drawer was the only one that was locked.

The mechanism was a simple single-bar mortice. It took the Saint precisely one minute to open it, thirty seconds of which were taken up with the bending of a large paper clip into the required angles.

The drawer contained only two items. One was a half-empty box of .22 cartridges. The other was a tooled black leather case about the same size as a canteen of cutlery with the initials *D.R.* worked into a gold-leaf monogram on the lid.

Simon flicked up the gilt clasp. Inside, the case was lined with purple felt and fitted with small square and rectangular mouldings strategically placed to hold the contents secure. Only the pistol they were designed to protect was missing.

As the Saint and every member of the newspaper-reading populace was aware, it was also a .22 which had terminated the earthly existence of Mr. Stanton Wakeforth.

At which point the average sleuth could have been pardoned for shouting "Eureka" and beating the world sprint record to take his discovery to the nearest police station. Simon Templar, however, considered his find with the cool detachment of a professional.

One .22-calibre bullet looks the same as any other .22-calibre bullet, and only tests carried out by a ballistics expert can determine whether they have both been fired from the same gun. The Saint had no doubt that within a short time the police would have made the comparisons and decided whether the same weapon was used to murder both Stanton Wakeforth and Colonel Harker. Therefore the only new ray of light he could cast on the investigations was to announce that Professor Rosco owned a .22 target pistol, but as British law requires all firearms to be licensed the police would very soon know that too—even if they did not know it already. And there must have been many other .22 guns in Cambridge. Which meant that to tell Superintendent Nutkin what he had found would only result in having to explain what he was doing near Bucksberry that morning, as well as burglarising Rosco's study. If he had found the pistol things might have been different, as it would then have been possible to discover whether it was used to fire the shots. But the pistol was not there, and neither was Professor Rosco.

He had still not found a connecting link between the three murders, and without that he had no way of guessing whether and where the murderer might strike again.

What little he had discovered had been largely the result of waiting on events and backing an instinct sharpened by many years of adventuring. He decided to keep to the same route.

He wiped off the box of cartridges and the pistol case, replaced them in the drawer, and relocked it. He doubted that the room had any more secrets to reveal, and with a final lingering look around and a rapid polishing of other things he had touched to remove his own fingerprints, he left the study.

He was retracing his steps towards the college gates when he turned a corner and almost collided with the hurrying person of Godfrey Nyall.

The bursar stepped back abruptly with a surprised expression. He looked as if he had dressed hastily that morning. The scuffed shoes, the sag in the knot of his tie, and his rumpled clothes were in contrast to the neatly attired man who had appeared at the hotel the previous morning and later dispensed sherry in the common room.

"Mr. Templar!" he exclaimed rather breathlessly. "I didn't know you were in the college."

Simon had been thinking of seeking out the bursar before leaving St. Enoch's.

"Actually I was looking for you," he lied smoothly. "But I couldn't find your office."

"It's near the main entrance," said Nyall. "You must have passed it when you came in."

The Saint smiled disarmingly.

"How silly of me. Can you spare a few minutes?"

The bursar hesitated for only a moment and then nodded.

"Of course. I just have to collect something from the common room. Perhaps you would wait for me in my office."

"Sure," said the Saint, and strolled away, conscious as he did so that the bursar had not moved and was watching him go.

As Nyall had said, it would have been hard to use the main entrance and miss his office. There were in fact two offices, an outer one with a desk for a secretary and beyond that the bursar's own sanctum. The typewriter was hooded and the desk top beside it bare, suggesting that the secretary, like the students, was on holiday. Nyall's office was spacious and imposing in the severe Victorian manner of large mahogany furniture and dark-coloured carpet. Those walls not hidden behind lattice-fronted bookcases were adorned with portraits in carved wooden frames and a few landscape prints in gilt surrounds.

The Saint perched on the edge of the leather-topped desk and glanced at the papers spread across it. They were mainly the heavier dailies plus a scattering of financial publications.

As he had not had a chance to read the morning papers, he selected one at random and began to flick idly through the pages. A column on the front page given over to the murder of Wakeforth and the Santa Claus link with the murder of Lazentree related that there had been no fresh developments. Inside the Saint found little to interest him, but he noted that the contents had certainly been of interest to someone, presumably Nyall.

In both the political and financial sections certain paragraphs, and in some instances whole stories, had been ringed in blue pencil. Political unrest in one of the South American banana—or in this case coffee—republics, news of a drought in West Africa, and conversely of a flood in East Africa, were marked, as were a feature article on the effects of strikes in United States copper mines and a speculative piece on the size of the following year's cocoa bean harvest.

Simon put the paper down and stood up. As he did so a photograph hanging on the wall near the desk caught his eye, and he walked over and studied it more closely. It showed a dozen soldiers in tropical kit standing and sitting in what appeared to be a jungle clearing. The men had the grim, weary eyes of seasoned soldiers in wartime which overshadowed the smiles they had offered the cameraman. Neither the location nor the date nor the identities of those shown was given but despite the years that had passed since its taking there was no mistaking Godfrey Nyall. He stood in the centre of the group, his slouch hat pushed back off his forehead, leaning on the barrel of his rifle. The soldier was slimmer, straighter, and harder than the man he had grown into, but there was the same strict look about the eyes and the same purposeful chiselling of nose and mouth. Simon looked for signs of his rank and found none. His companions also wore no indication of their status, which made the Saint even more curious. There was an explanation nagging at the back of his memory but refusing to formulate itself.

He was still puzzling over the picture when the door opened and he turned to greet the bursar.

"I'm sorry to have kept you waiting," said Nyall. "Have you found out anything more about the murder of Sir Basil?"

"Only that he was due to meet Stanton Wakeforth at 3:30 P.M. today," said the Saint, finally deciding that the time had come to make use of the clue he had found in the store tycoon's diary. "Do you know why?"

Nyall's brow furrowed and he slowly shook his head.

"He told me nothing about it," he replied at length. "I didn't even know they were acquainted. But then unless it had some direct bearing on St. Enoch's funds there would have been no reason for me to be informed."

"I take it that you are responsible for the college coffers," said the Saint.

"Of course, it is my main responsibility," Nyall answered as he went behind his desk and sat down. "We are not a wealthy college like some others in Cambridge, but there are still substantial amounts involved."

"Mainly government grants, bequests, donations, that kind of thing?" Simon hazarded.

"Mainly," Nyall agreed. "But there are investments to be considered as well."

"Stocks and shares, you mean?"

Nyall's lips broke in a brief, almost patronising smile.

"Nothing exciting, I'm afraid. Mainly long-dated government bonds, gilts, a small portfolio of some of the blue chip companies," he said dismissively. "We can't afford to be gamblers."

The Saint nodded.

"No, I suppose not. Will Sir Basil's death affect the finances at all?"

Nyall tidied up the papers and placed them in a pile on one side of the desk while he replied.

"No, I should think not, at least in the short term. Of course, he was a well-known man, and a figurehead always helps to make a college better known generally and so leads to more donations."

There was a rap on the door and Dr. Burridge entered. He looked uncertainly from Nyall to the Saint.

"Good morning, Mr. Templar. I'm sorry, Godfrey, I didn't realise you were busy. I'll return later."

"Don't go on my account," said the Saint, who had glimpsed Chantek crossing the courtyard outside. "I was just about to leave anyway."

It was nearly the truth and the sight of Chantek had made it so. Within the college walls he felt unnaturally cramped, and although there were still questions he wished to ask he would prefer to put them on his own or neutral ground.

"I was wondering," he continued pleasantly, "if you gentlemen could have lunch with me. Perhaps you would also invite Professor Darslow and Professor Rosco. Since you invited me to apply myself to the recent goings-on, I've had some more thoughts which might be worth kicking around."

Both men looked at each other as if hoping the other would make the first refusal. The Saint could sense that neither found the invitation overwelcome but both appeared at a loss for a plausible excuse. He looked at his watch and saw that it still needed a few minutes to noon.

"Shall we say one o'clock at my hotel?" he asked.

Nyall nodded mutely. Burridge's voice was strained.

"That is very kind of you."

"I hope you'll still think so this afternoon," said the Saint cordially.

He caught up with Chantek on the far side of the quadrangle.

"What have you been doing?" she asked eagerly.

"Just nosing around," he said evasively. "I found some circumstantial evidence, which is notoriously unreliable. So I won't confuse you with it in advance. Meanwhile, you are invited to lunch."

He explained who would be there, and Chantek looked as uneasy at the prospect as Burridge and Nyall had done. She did not relish the idea of being surrounded by those who had seemed like demigods for most of the year. But the Saint brushed aside her fears and after making her promise not to be late drove back to the University Arms.

He felt as if he had already done a full day's work, and welcomed the reviving properties of a shower and a change of clothes. He was unhappily contemplating the imminent obligation to select a necktie when the telephone rang.

The voice on the other end of the line was brisk and businesslike.

"Mr. Templar?"

Simon admitted his identity and enquired that of his caller.

"My name is Casden. Brian Casden. I run a company called Happy Time Toys."

"Sounds like fun," said the Saint.

Casden ignored the interpolation and continued: "I understand you are investigating the murders of Sir Basil Lazentree and Stanton Wakeforth."

"You could say I'm slightly involved," the Saint admitted guardedly. "Why?"

There was a lengthy pause before the question was answered, and then Casden's voice sounded strained.

"I think I may be next."

8

Simon Templar frequently found his reputation a hindrance. Fame, he sometimes felt, brought with it more problems than an already overworked outlaw should reasonably be asked to contend with, and he could become wistful for the days when only a small privileged band of fellow adventurers had known his baptismal name, and the world outside heard only of a mysterious figure who passed like an avenging wraith across the paths of the unrighteous.

But notoriety also had its advantages. Fate had obligingly delivered him to the right spot at the correct o'clock, but the aura surrounding his name had done much of the rest. Without it, Superintendent Nutkin might have treated him with less undeserved suspicion and more civility and thereby not invited him to puncture the detective's pomposity. Without it, Godfrey Nyall would not have approached him and he would not so easily have made the acquaintance of the St. Enoch hierarchy. And without it Brian Casden would not have telephoned and held out a possible solution to the mystery.

With a slow pensive smile the Saint relaxed into a chair and rested his feet on the counterpane of the bed.

"You don't say?" he drawled. "And why should you consider yourself the next candidate for the hereafter?"

Again several seconds of silence passed while Brian Casden carefully shaped his reply. The businessman's natural caution vying with personal anxiety, Simon thought. He waited patiently, confident that, having decided to make contact, the other would not hang up now.

"Sir Basil and I were discussing a donation to the college," Casden said finally. "When he was murdered I didn't imagine for a moment that it had anything to do with our plans. Stanton Wakeforth was also involved and when he was killed I began to wonder. It seemed like too much of a coincidence. But now that Harker has been murdered . . ."

"How did you know Colonel Harker was dead?" Simon cut in quickly.

"It was on the radio news. Nothing much, just that a report has been received that he had been shot while hunting."

The Saint nodded to himself, satisfied with the explanation. The murder had taken place early enough for word of it to have reached the reporters who were already in Cambridge following up the previous killings.

He returned to his original line of questioning.

"What exactly were the four of you planning?"

"Wakeforth and I were to endow a new faculty for business studies."

"And Colonel Harker?"

"He owns—owned—some land near the college. He was

prepared to let St. Enoch's have it at a nominal price providing his company was given the building contract."

All of which, Simon judged, made sense. Even if it still did not provide him with the motive he sought, it did at least link the three dead men.

"Have you spoken to the police yet?" he asked.

"No."

It was too curt an answer to pass unchallenged.

"Why not?"

"I didn't want to get involved," said Casden hesitantly. "It wouldn't be good publicity for a company such as ours. I had read that you were investigating and I thought I would talk to you first. One of the stories in the newspapers mentioned where you were staying."

Again the Saint was satisfied with the explanation.

"Tell me," he said thoughtfully. "You say you have been discussing all this with Sir Basil and the other two—for how long?"

"Since October, soon after Sir Basil came to Cambridge. It was all finally agreed last week, and we were due to sign the necessary papers tomorrow."

"On Christmas Eve? Why the rush?"

"Both my company and Wakeforth's end our financial years on January 31," Casden replied. "There were certain tax advantages to be considered regarding the funds we were making available."

"And who else knew about these plans of yours?"

As he put the question Simon heard other voices in the background and guessed that Casden was no longer alone. The businessman's sudden vagueness confirmed the impression.

"I can't go into details now," he answered abruptly.

"How soon can we meet?" Simon asked.

"Come to my office at six this evening."

The Saint consulted his watch.

"That gives you five and a quarter hours in which to get yourself killed," he pointed out.

"I can't see you before then."

Casden sounded irritable, and the volume of background noise suggested that his company had increased. Without prompting he continued: "Every year we hold a Christmas party in our canteen for deprived children. It's this afternoon. I shan't be free until six, but I also won't be alone."

The Saint was unimpressed by the degree of safety such a gathering would provide and sensed that Casden too was more hopeful than confident. But at least he was prepared for danger, which was an advantage none of the others had enjoyed.

"Where is your office?" Simon asked resignedly, convinced by the other's tone that there would be little point in pressing for an earlier meeting.

Casden told him and the Saint repeated the directions, both to confirm them and to commit them to memory.

The hubbub surrounding his caller had grown so loud that it threatened to drown Casden's voice completely.

"I must go now," he said firmly.

The Saint sighed.

"Don't talk to any strange Santas," he advised, but the line was dead before he finished speaking.

Simon returned to the adjusting of his tie and thought through what Casden had told him. What interested him most of all was not what had been said but what had not been said. Casden had been unresponsive when asked who else knew what was being planned. If he had thought nobody else was involved he could have said so without giving anything away to those around him. But he had chosen to refuse to talk, which meant that he knew that somebody else knew but didn't want to reveal who it was. As to whether that person was a suspected murderer or a potential victim he had offered no clue.

The Saint was slipping on his jacket when the telephone buzzed again, but this time it was just to inform him that Chantek had arrived.

He walked down to the lobby, looking in at the private room he had booked an hour before to check that all was as it should be. It was, and so was Chantek. He kissed her lightly on the forehead and smiled at the nervousness in her eyes.

"Don't worry, they're not ogres," he reassured her as he led the way back up the stairs, adding mischievously: "Well, not all of them."

She pouted.

"It's all right for you. I have to return to St. Enoch's in January. You don't."

"January is another year," Simon said airily. "Personally I rarely plan beyond tomorrow. Sufficient unto the day, et cetera. And the day has hardly begun."

They were taking the first sips of their respective aperitifs, hers a vermouth, his a pink gin, when Darslow arrived. He hovered a step inside the room and eyed them uncertainly.

"Dr. Burridge said I was invited." He made it sound like an apology.

"And so you are, Edwin, old thing," Simon confirmed with a grin.

He ordered a large measure of malt to top up the professor's already high spirit level. Judging by his breath and slightly rolling gait, Darslow must have been drinking steadily since he had left Chantek over an hour earlier.

Darslow cupped the tumbler in both hands and gulped at the contents.

"What's happened?" he asked in an attempt at a conspiratorial whisper that came out loud enough to be heard in the back row of the stalls.

The Saint smiled.

"If you mean has anything new occurred to affect you in connection with this morning's shenanigans, then the answer is nothing."

Darslow looked blank.

"Then why do you want me here?"

Simon patted him encouragingly between the shoulder blades as he guided him towards a chair.

"Because I like you, Edwin," he responded with a bonhomie that made Darslow peer at him in bleary-eyed suspicion. "I want you to tell me all about codicils and torts and Gintrap v. Gintrap 1929, and fascinating things like that."

He motioned to the waiter at the side table that was serving as a bar to top up his guest's glass. Darslow drunk, he decided, might be more interesting than Darslow sober. Without the stimulus of alcohol he was likely to repeat his nervous seat-perching silences of the previous evening, whereas once sufficiently lubricated there was always the chance that he might inadvertently contribute something of interest to the debate.

Leaving Chantek to keep him company, the Saint turned to greet the arrival of Dr. Burridge and Godfrey Nyall.

"Good of you to come, gentlemen."

"Kind of you to invite us, Mr. Templar," the dean rejoined stiffly.

"Most kind," echoed Nyall.

"And Professor Rosco?" Simon asked.

"I'm afraid we could not locate him," said Burridge.

"He hasn't been in the college all morning," added Nyall. "We left a message in his study in case he returned."

If the Saint was disappointed at the non-appearance of the man he most wanted to meet he did not allow it to show.

"Perhaps he may come along later," he said, and proceeded to introduce the two men to Chantek, whom Nyall admitted to knowing by sight but whom the dean could not recall at all, and then to administer to their liquid needs.

From that moment until most of the meal was consumed the Saint guided the conversation along paths that had nothing to do with the events that had brought them together. He was the perfect host, seeing to the requirements of his guests, listening and chatting and allowing them their silences. Once or twice he caught Chantek's eye and smiled at her puzzled expression. She had expected some sort of interrogation, not a convivial get-together. But the Saint knew exactly what he was doing.

They talked about student grants, speculated on the likely repercussions of government cuts in the education budget, recalled places they had visited and people they had met, and gradually the atmosphere thawed until by the time the plates were pushed towards the centre of the table the gathering almost resembled that of old friends.

The process was helped by the standard of the cuisine, which was better than the Saint had hoped, and the quality of the wines, which were everything he expected. The fact that Darslow swallowed the vintage Lafite as if it were lager and threatened at any moment to slide from view added to rather than subtracted from the relaxed mood around the table.

Finally, when the cheeseboard was in place and the port circulated, he brought the conversation adroitly around to the subjects that most interested him. He had casually enquired about the process of appointing a new Master for the college, and the dean had explained about the make-up of the committee that would make the decision.

"I expect we shall convene in the New Year," said Burridge. "It would not do to go too long without a Master."

"But surely it's merely an honorary post," said the Saint. "The college can function from day to day whether there is a Master or not."

Burridge shook his head and smiled thinly as he leant his elbows on the table and placed his fingertips together in a mannerism Simon had noticed him employ several times during the course of the lunch whenever he wished to emphasise a point.

"To be the Master of St. Enoch's is an honour of course, but though in some colleges the Master might be just a figurehead, this is not the case at St. Enoch's," the dean explained. "The tradition here is that the Master has almost total executive control. It comes down to us from the time when the places of learning were controlled by monks who would unquestionably obey their abbot."

"You mean that once appointed he can do anything he likes?" Simon asked in mild surprise.

Nyall answered: "Almost, yes. But of course there are limits, even if they are broad ones."

"Supposing a Master wanted to do something which the other fellows objected to," suggested the Saint. "Could you get it thrown out or would you have to like it or lump it?"

"Usually a compromise is reached," Burridge said. "If the Master had all the staff against him, the difficulties that would be put in his way would be such that it is doubtful if he could carry on in the face of their opposition."

"But if some were for and some against, it would be possible, I suppose," said the Saint.

"I suppose it would," Burridge agreed. "But the situation is hardly likely to arise."

Simon studied the dean's face as he pursued his questioning and was conscious of the man's strength. Not in the physical sense, though his frame was wiry enough to make him powerful above the average, but rather his force of will. He might speak slowly and pedantically but the words were underscored by an inner strength and always there was the hint of a fire behind the eyes and a tension in the long-fingered hands which belied his outward calm.

"Last night you mentioned that you objected to some of Sir Basil's plans for the future of the college," Simon reminded him. "Couldn't those plans have led to just such a situation?"

"That question is now, alas, academic," put in Nyall, but the Saint ignored him and continued to concentrate his attention on the dean.

"But couldn't they?" he repeated.

"It is possible," Burridge admitted.

"You didn't like Sir Basil, did you, Dr. Burridge?"

Simon's tone was even and the very directness of the question robbed it of offence.

The dean returned the Saint's stare and for several seconds the two men appraised each other in a silence that grew steadily more tense.

"I had nothing against him personally," said Burridge at last, and there was a new and harsher edge to his voice. "But I most certainly did not like what he was planning to do to St. Enoch's."

Burridge paused and the others round the table waited for him to continue. When he did so the even tenor of his speech was quickly shaken and then broke completely, and what began as an explanation rapidly turned into an impassioned diatribe.

"I have seen his like too many times before. I have seen what they've done to other colleges. I didn't want him here but I was overruled. I feared for the future of St. Enoch's. Sir Basil and his so-called progressive ideas would have been the ruin of the college, as has happened elsewhere. Once the colleges of Cambridge and Oxford were seats of learning, of intellectual debate and reasoning. We produced scholars of the arts, great philosophers, statesmen, men who shaped and expanded the culture of the world. But not now. Once knowledge was the goal; not now. Now all that matters is the degree, a slip of parchment, a ticket to halfway up the executive ladder. Instead of scholars we produce salesmen. Instead of broadening minds we are narrowing them, channelling them for a specific use, turning out fuel for the furnaces of commerce and industry, all in the hallowed name of progress. Progress to what? That's a question Sir Basil and his like never stop to consider. Bigger. Better. Newer. That's all they worry about. Well, it may be all very well for the modern universities to follow the trend. But not Cambridge. That was not why we were founded, that is not why we have survived, and that is not how we are going to continue to survive."

Throughout his speech the Saint had never taken his eyes off the dean and had felt the heat of the fire that flared in the man's eyes and the force of emotion behind the unconscious clenching and unclenching of his hands. The silence that followed his tirade was as brittle as glass; even the waiters clearing away the bar had stopped to listen.

Only one man seemed unaffected, and it was he who shattered the quiet. Edwin Darslow giggled.

"Hear, hear," he chuckled. "Quite right. Don't want to get a name for turning out economists and people like that, do we? Eh, Nyall?"

The Saint looked quizzically at the bursar, who coloured slightly beneath his gaze.

"I think Professor Darslow has overenjoyed your hospitality, Mr. Templar," Nyall remarked acidly. "The fact that I have a degree in economics has always been a strange source of amusement to the professor."

"Always telling other people what to do with their money, but never doing it themselves," retorted Darslow. "Like racing tipsters. If they were any good they'd back the horses themselves, not tell other people about them."

Darslow tapped the side of his nose with his finger in an exaggerated gesture of conspiratorial wisdom.

"Physician, heal thyself," he lisped. "*Iatre, therapeuson seauton.*"

His display of erudition was somewhat marred by his enunciation, which phoneticised the transliterated Greek according to the atrocious British academic tradition, and with the accent invariably in the wrong places. Neither St. Luke nor Archbishop Makarios would have had the faintest idea what he was trying to say.

Had Chantek not slipped a restraining arm beneath his shoulder as he began to slip forward he would have crumpled gently to the floor. As she pulled him into a more upright pose he emitted a loud snore.

The dean regarded him with distaste.

"Dreadful. Quite dreadful."

"I think perhaps we had better get Professor Darslow home," suggested Nyall.

The Saint nodded sympathetically.

"I think you had," he agreed.

He was not sorry that the party was breaking up. He had gleaned more than he had originally hoped. He helped Nyall get Darslow downstairs and loaded into a taxi. The dean walked a few paces behind as if trying to dissociate himself from them. They said their goodbyes and thanks on the pavement, and Simon returned upstairs to Chantek.

"Will Professor Darslow be all right?" she asked.

He smiled.

"Fine, but I wouldn't like to have his head when he wakes up."

Chantek's eyes roamed over the remains of the luncheon table.

"I was surprised at Dr. Burridge," she said. "He was so angry. He almost made me feel afraid."

"Yes, it was an interesting little revelation, wasn't it?" he agreed thoughtfully.

"What do we do now?" Chantek asked.

He looked at his watch. It was almost three-thirty, still

two and a half hours before his appointment with Brian Casden.

"Let's get some fresh air. A walk around town to get rid of some of the calories is called for. I may even get around to buying some Christmas presents."

"Not from a Santa, I hope," she laughed.

The Saint smiled as he slipped his arm through hers.

"No, definitely not from a Santa," he agreed.

9

The dashboard clock showed one minute to six when the Hirondel drew up to the gates of the Happy Time Toy Co. The Saint sounded the klaxon and the strident blast brought a figure in blue uniform and peaked cap from a kiosk just the other side of the barrier.

Simon spoke to the man from his driving seat.

"I have an appointment with Mr. Casden."

"Name?"

Simon told him, and the man checked it against the sheet of paper on his clipboard.

"Drive round to the side of the building over there, Mr. Casden's office is on the top floor. Can't miss it."

The Saint did as he was instructed, driving slowly and taking in the topography as he followed the road around, and braked outside a door marked STAFF ENTRANCE.

The factory and offices of the Happy Time Toy Co. were situated on a new industrial estate on the edge of the city. The factory comprised three linked single-storey buildings that reminded him of aircraft hangars. The offices were housed in a three-storey block of concrete and glass tacked onto the end nearest the gates.

A high wire-mesh fence encircled the site, dividing it from the road at the front and similar style factories on either side, and a few rubble-strewn acres at the rear where another factory was being built. It certainly looked secure enough.

He had spent the afternoon with Chantek wandering around the Cambridge shops and finally being fleeced for an afternoon tea of scones and jam in a dimly lit shoppe where the cost was in inverse proportion to the height of the ceiling. They had talked no further of the murders. The Saint had long since cultivated the ability to switch off his problems and relax in the same way that he could sleep at any time like a cat. Now, after the breathing space he had permitted himself, his thoughts were completely back with the matter in hand.

He climbed out of the car and tried the door. It was unlocked. Both factory and offices appeared to be totally deserted. He followed the stairs up to the top-floor landing without meeting anyone. The lack of any form of security, even the most ancient of night watchmen, worried him. In ordinary circumstances he would have expected to be challenged. And these were not ordinary circumstances.

As the guard on the gate had said, it would have been difficult to miss Casden's office, which stood at the end of the corridor. But there was an additional reason why it could not be overlooked that night.

The watchman lay face down across the closed doorway.

Simon knelt and searched for a pulse. He smiled grimly as his fingers located the tiny beat. It was weak, but not dangerously so. There was no wound to be seen, only a rapidly swelling purple bruise on the side of the man's neck.

The Saint straightened up and as he did so his fingers slipped under his left cuff and drew out the throwing knife that was strapped along his forearm. He had not brought a gun with him and events had moved too quickly to allow him to return to London to fetch one. He was not unduly concerned. He could do tricks with that six-inch blade that would have won him top billing in any circus. And if a reception committee was waiting for him he was sure that it had a membership of no more than one.

His hand closed on the door handle and stayed there for a moment while he listened for any sound of movement on the other side of the door. Hearing nothing, he turned the handle and went in.

A man who could only have been Brian Casden lay in a similar pose to that of his employee outside, except for the red pool that spread from the left side of his body. This time Simon did not bother to feel for a sign of life. Casden lay a few feet inside his secretary's office, and the Saint had to step over his body to enter the room beyond. It was empty, and he sheathed his knife.

He stood for a while in the open doorway between the two offices and appraised the scene. It was clear at a glance how the murder had happened. It was the oldest trick in the oldest book since Genesis. Which was probably why it so often worked so well. Casden had heard a noise in the outer office and had gone to investigate. The murderer had waited behind the door, and Casden probably never knew what hit him.

But what was even more interesting was the fact that the contents of the personal filing cabinet behind Casden's desk were scattered across the carpet. The killer had lingered long enough to remove some evidence. And that confirmed the Saint in his belief that Casden had known more than he had said on the telephone.

There were three telephones on the secretary's desk. At the second attempt he found the one with an outside line and dialled the police. He asked for Superintendent Nutkin.

He grinned as the detective came on the line.

"Hullo, Nutcase," he murmured. "This is Simon Templar. I've got another body for you."

"You've got a *what?*" Nutkin almost shouted.

"A body. You know, a corpse, a late-lamented, a cadaver, a dearly departed, a . . ."

"Who, for God's sake?" Nutkin's voice gave the impression that he was being strangled.

"Brian Casden. Late boss man of the Happy Time Toy Co."

"Templar, if this is some kind of a joke—"

"Oh, it's hysterically funny," said the Saint caustically. "Dear old Brian is laughing himself silly, or he would be if someone hadn't shoved a knife into his back."

He dropped the handset back into its cradle. Instinct told him that little was likely to be gained by searching the office. But it might be interesting to see if there were any clues to how the killer got in.

Outside, the watchman was still sleeping and Simon did not disturb him. He made his way down to the ground level and walked across to the gate.

"Did Mr. Casden have any visitors before me?" he asked the guard.

The man's automatic reaction was to be officious. Then

he looked at the stern set of the Saint's features and wisely decided to be cooperative.

"Not since the children left, and that was about half an hour ago."

"What about the staff?"

"They all had the afternoon off, except for those who volunteered to help with the party."

"And you saw them all leave?"

"Yes. What's all this about?"

"You'll find out very soon," Simon told him, and turned on his heel to walk briskly along the line of the fence.

He found what he was searching for at the rear of the site: a large hole clipped through the mesh almost at ground level. And he found something else too. Caught on a sharp strand of wire was a tatter of red cloth. The Saint left it alone. It was something that Nutkin would be able to slip into a plastic bag and label as evidence. He would like that.

The Saint strolled back to the office block. So Santa had turned up despite Casden's belief in his security, had done what he had come to do, and slipped away again. A children's party must have seemed an irresistible opportunity and he had not missed it.

"But have I missed mine?" Simon asked himself as he re-entered Casden's office.

He stood and looked down at the murdered man. On impulse he abandoned his previous intention of leaving the body alone and quickly rifled the pockets. In Casden's jacket was a small leather-bound address book. Wakeforth, Harker, and Sir Basil were among the entries.

"And who else?" wondered the Saint as he slid the book into his own pocket.

And then came the pounding of heavy boots in the corridor, and with a resigned sigh he turned to greet Superintendent Nutkin.

The following hours were little more than a playback of the sequences that had followed the deaths of Lazentree and Wakeforth. Nutkin asked and Simon answered with discretion; Simon asked and Nutkin refused to answer. At the end of it all, the detective knew about Casden's phone call but nothing about the plan to enlarge the college, he knew about the lunch party but not what had been said, and he knew everything about the finding of the body except for the address book that Simon had taken into his own safekeeping. And the Saint knew absolutely nothing about the detective's own enquiries—which, he reckoned, made them about even.

The Saint's own innocence had been established by the watchman, who came to a few minutes after the police arrived only to tell them that he had seen and heard nothing. He had been making a routine tour of the building when he had been hit from behind. All he could be definite about was the time, ten minutes before the Saint passed through the main gate—when, as Simon offered to prove, he had only just left Chantek.

And so, at last, the Saint was allowed to go on his way. But by that time there was nowhere else to go except back to the hotel, where the dining room had closed and the best the night staff could provide in the way of fodder was a round of ham sandwiches.

It had started snowing again midway through the evening, and the Saint lay in bed watching the flakes drift past his window and thinking back over all that had happened. He cursed himself for not having insisted on seeing Casden earlier but was slightly comforted by a hunch that told him that somewhere in everything he had seen and heard was to be found the last piece of the puzzle.

He had long since eliminated Darslow from his list of suspects. Not only could he absolve the professor of Harker's murder, but he reckoned that Darslow would still have been sleeping off the effects of his drinking spree when Casden had been done in. That left Denzil Rosco, Dr. Burridge, and Godfrey Nyall.

Simon considered each in turn.

Rosco had been unseen for the whole day. He had the ability and the opportunity to kill Harker and Casden. But did he have any motive? He appeared to have liked the shake-up that Sir Basil's arrival at St. Enoch's had foreshadowed. So why kill him? On the other hand, it was almost certainly his gun that had despatched two of the victims. And the gun was missing. But then, why not shoot Casden instead of knifing him? Only Rosco could provide any of the answers, and Rosco wasn't around to do so.

Burridge had shown signs of being a fanatic. And fanatics are always dangerous. His adherence to tradition and hatred of progress were clearly deep-rooted. But strong enough to force him to kill, not once but four times in as many days? He had been in London when Sir Basil and Stanton Wakeforth died, an easier place in which to set up an alibi than Cambridge. What had he been doing that morning and afternoon and could it be checked out? The Saint made a mental memo to give that an early priority.

And then there was Nyall. He appeared to have no axe worth grinding. But there was something about him which still didn't quite fit. What was it Darslow had said? "Physician, heal thyself. . . . Like a racing tipster." An interesting comparison. The Saint added another mental note to ask Darslow for clarification.

"But there's still something I must have overlooked, something so obvious that it's blinding," he told himself as he slipped into sleep.

He repeated the thought to Chantek the following midday over sausages and mash at the Crown. The press corps camped in the hotel lobby had become an increasing irritant, and even before the manager tactfully suggested that he might be more comfortable elsewhere he had decided to move. The Crown had been his immediate choice. It was off the main track yet could not have been nearer the college. And if the room and the food did not match the hotel's standards, at least the management was friendly and he could come and go without subterfuge.

Chantek was idly toying with her knife as she listened to his account of the previous evening's events. Suddenly he stopped and stared at her.

"Do that again," he ordered.

She looked blank.

"Do what again?"

"Hold the knife the way you held it just now."

Chantek obeyed as if preparing to cut off a piece of sausage.

"Now hold it as if you were going to stab me from behind."

"Why?" Chantek asked in surprise.

"Never mind," said the Saint. "Just do it."

She reversed her grip on the handle, so that the blade projected beyond her little finger, raising her hand to head level as if to bring the point slashing downwards.

"Exactly," Simon said triumphantly.

"Exactly what?" demanded Chantek, growing impatient with the game.

"Exactly the way any amateur would do it. But not the way a professional would do it. Casden was killed by somebody who knew his business. And there aren't so many people around who know how to use a knife properly."

"How do you mean, 'properly'?"

"Your way would come down between the shoulder blades and probably miss any vital organs. An expert holds a knife pointing forward, something like a rapier, with his thumb on the flat of the blade to guide it." He demonstrated. "Insert between the ribs at the right angle: knife pierces heart, victim dead in seconds."

Chantek shuddered.

"How horrible!"

"But effective, very effective," said the Saint. "And that is how Casden was killed. And men who are experts in that particular field usually have some special background in common."

He stood up directly they had finished their plates. He seemed somehow larger than life, colder and more impersonal than the winter outside. There were still many things he did not understand, but at last he had a positive clue to follow and little doubt that it would lead him to his goal.

With the briefest of apologies for his sudden departure and a promise to call her later, he left Chantek and headed for the college.

In the entrance hallway he met Professor Darslow, who looked at him sheepishly and began to stammer excuses for his behaviour the previous day. Simon cut him short.

"Never mind that now. You said something about

Nyall. 'Physician, heal thyself.' What were you getting at?"

"I think I remember," Darslow replied uncertainly. "It was a joke, really. Godfrey is always advising people about shares to buy. It's just a bit of a joke that if he's so clever why isn't he rich? That's all."

"Aren't his tips any good?"

"I don't really know. I haven't followed them."

"Then you don't actually know that he isn't rich," said the Saint provocatively.

He left the professor and hurried to the bursar's office. It was locked. He was considering picking the lock when another thought came to him. He went back to Darslow.

"Where is Sir Basil's office?" he asked.

"First floor, almost directly above us. Why?"

"Tell you later," said the Saint, the words floating over his shoulder as he took the stairs three at a time.

The office of the Master of St. Enoch's College was unlocked but not empty. Professor Denzil Rosco turned in surprise as Simon swept into the room.

"Good afternoon," said the Saint evenly. "Found anything interesting?"

Rosco looked up from the open drawers of the desk by which he was standing.

"I suppose this appears rather suspicious," he admitted with a wry smile. "Well, the police have just been trying to nail me for murder, so I suppose breaking and entering will be considered small cheese after that."

The Saint perched himself on the edge of the desk.

"Tell me about it," he invited.

Rosco obliged. He had spent the day and night before with friends, completely unaware of what had happened until he had returned that morning to find a policeman waiting for him in his rooms. He had been informed that his pistol had been used to kill Lazentree and Wakeforth. The police had searched his study and found it.

The Saint interrupted.

"They found the pistol in your study?"

"Yes. Why?"

"Never mind. Carry on."

Rosco carried on. He had tried to explain that anyone could have taken it, but Nutkin had not been impressed. Only when his alibi had been checked had the superintendent reluctantly allowed him to leave.

"So what exactly are you doing here?" Simon wanted to know.

"Clutching at straws," Rosco replied with a sigh. "But I thought it was worth a try."

"What was?"

"Sir Basil and I became friendly very quickly. We both had similar ideas about St. Enoch's, which made us both unpopular in certain quarters."

"What did he tell you?"

Rosco shrugged.

"Not much, but he hinted. Said he'd got the financial backing for his plans. Businessmen, from what I could gather, but he didn't say who. Said he was planning a *fait accompli* to present to the others in the New Year. He was very excited about it."

Rosco paused and seemed less confident of himself when he continued.

"I started thinking about what you said about motive. Could someone have found out about it and killed him to stop it happening? It seemed absurd, but I couldn't get the idea out of my mind. If that *was* possible, then mightn't Wakeforth be one of the businessmen? Couldn't

Casden and Harker also have been involved? I thought I'd see if there was any sort of clue in Basil's office."

The Saint regarded him with respect.

"Professor, you must have your eye on Nutkin's job," he said. "But finding out who was backing Basil wouldn't point to who killed him."

"Then what are you doing here?"

Simon produced Casden's address book.

"I thought I'd see if they had any other chums in common, which might point to another possible murderer. Then I could watch him until the murderer tries for another killing." He looked at the young man keenly. "Are you sure Basil never mentioned any names?"

Rosco's brow furrowed as he thought. At last he said: "Yes, there was someone, but I can't quite remember. It was someone in the House of Lords who was going to lend his name to whatever Basil was planning. It would add some distinction, he said."

Simon flicked through the address book. It was hardly Debrett's. Two Sirs were the best he could find until he came to the *G*'s.

"Grantchester. Lord Grantchester. How does that sound?"

Rosco nodded.

"That's it. I'm sure of it. I knew there was a local connection but I couldn't think what."

"What's the betting our noble lord is next on the list?" Simon mused as he lifted the telephone and gave the number from Casden's book to the operator.

He waited impatiently until she came back to say that the number of unobtainable. Last night's storm, he was informed, had brought down the overhead lines. Reconnection was not expected until after Christmas holiday.

"By which time Lord Grantchester is likely to be as cold as tomorrow's turkey," Simon observed.

"I'll contact the police," Rosco was saying as he reached to take over the telephone. But the Saint stopped him.

"Why should we let the superintendent have all the fun? I consider this a very personal party."

Five minutes later he was pointing the long nose of the Hirondel down the ice-coated road towards Grantchester.

10

The weather is the favourite conversational gambit among the English for one simple reason: they are always totally unprepared for it. In summer, a week of what in any Latin country would be regarded as pleasantly warm weather leads to newspaper headlines that cry "Heat Wave" and moves to ration water. In winter, what any Indian worth his monsoon would consider a fairly heavy shower results in radio warnings of bursting river banks and flooded homes. But these pale into insignificance beside the chaos produced by a few inches of snow. Roads are blocked, trains stop, and pipes burst. The populace gazes at the white crystal falling like magic from the sky and wonders at the fact that it is snowing in December, forgetting that they have been singing about dreaming of a white Christmas for most of the month.

So ran the Saint's thoughts as he grimly forced the Hirondel towards its destination.

The worst of the storm had passed before first light and by midday had subsided to brief flurries not heavy enough to fill a footprint. The volume of traffic had ensured that the town centre streets remained clear, but once the outskirts were reached the going became steadily slower. And if the outskirts were bad the cross-country roads were worse. The main trunk route to London was passable with care, but the lanes leading to the villages it by-passes featured hard-packed ruts alternating with treacherous soft drifts.

The light was failing quickly as the sharp brightness of the afternoon gave way to twilight that hung like a blue-black backdrop against the whiteness of the land. The Hirondel's powerful headlamps carved a tunnel of brilliance through the gloom, and the Saint drove along it as fast as the conditions allowed, which was not breaking any records.

The broad tread of the Hirondel's winter tyres hugged the icy surface, giving him better control than most of the other traffic, but still the journey seemed to take an age. It was not so much the snow and ice themselves as the mishaps which had befallen other motorists that delayed him. A lorry loaded with bricks had failed to master an incline and had been abandoned while its driver went for help, causing a long tailback. Once that obstacle had been passed, it was found that a family car had managed to get stuck in a snowbank on the other side of the hill, and again he found himself obliged to join some other compulsory Samaritans in helping to dig it out and clear the blockage. And so it went on.

Grantchester lies just three miles from Cambridge but it was more than half an hour before the church tower came into view. He stopped outside the rectory in the main street and consulted his Ordnance Survey map. Blansdown Court, the country seat of Lord Grantchester, lay three miles farther on into the snow-carpeted countryside.

The holdups, although annoying, did give him time to marshal his thoughts.

He was playing a hunch, no more than that. Dr. Burridge had not been around that morning so the questions Simon wanted answers to had remained unasked. And as for Godfrey Nyall, his suspicion was based on only one foundation. Chantek's playing with her knife had jogged his memory and made him recall the picture he had seen in the bursar's study. The lack of identifications that had puzzled him were explained. That had been one of the rules of jungle warfare. Small groups working behind enemy lines, against the Japanese in Burma, had worn no badges of rank so that if captured the officers would not be identified. And they knew how to use a knife and were trained in unarmed combat to deliver the sort of blow that had felled Casden's watchman. But its feasibility alone was not enough. Burridge's fanatical conservatism was at least a motive of sorts. But outwardly Nyall appeared to have no reason to use any skills he might remember from his army service. Unless the Saint's other guess was correct. Perhaps Lord Grantchester could suggest the necessary link. But then, there was no real certainty that he was next in line for a requiem. And even if he was, that didn't mean that the danger was immediate. Reason told Simon that he could well be wasting his time; instinct told him to hurry. He pressed on.

Blansdown Court was as impressive a stately home as any day tripper in search of historical variety could have asked for. It rose from the flat Cambridgeshire farmlands in the centre of a spacious park surrounded on all sides by a crumbling grey brick wall. It was shaped like an E without the centre bar. The stem of the E was graceful white Georgian with an ornate portico reached by double flights of steps which met in front of it. The east wing, though trying to blend with the central block, appeared to have been built a century later. The west wing was the original Elizabethan manor house, its small red bricks fitted around angled beams as stout as ships' timbers, its tall chimneys leaning where the roof had sagged. The gateway was mid-Victorian Gothic. The tall iron gates were open. There were no signs of life in the lodges on either side.

The Saint drove through, followed the winding drive up to the house, and parked at the end of a row of half a dozen cars near the main steps.

His ring was answered by an elderly butler. Simon voiced his wish to see Lord Grantchester. No, he was not expected. The butler showed him into a small waiting room, enquired his name, and told him to wait while he checked with his lordship. He shuffled off across the cavernous high-domed hall and Simon followed soundlessly in his wake. He had no intention of hanging around only to be told that his lordship was not available.

The butler entered a room in a corridor leading from the hall. He delivered his message.

A voice said gruffly: "What does he want?"

"A few words," answered the Saint, walking in as if on cue.

He found himself in a pleasantly comfortable drawing room. Logs blazed in the Adam fireplace and in front of it four people were finishing their afternoon tea. The two eldest were obviously Lord and Lady Grantchester. The younger two looked as if they might be their son and daughter-in-law or vice versa.

"Excuse my abruptness, sir," said the Saint. "But the matter I have to discuss with you is very urgent."

His lordship peered at his visitor from beneath bushy white eyebrows that matched his thick white moustache. Simon placed him at around seventy, yet despite his age there was a certain strength and alertness about him. He sat waiting for an explanation, and Simon realised that his surname alone might not have been quite sufficient.

"My name is *Simon* Templar. You may have heard of me. I'm sometimes called the Saint."

The gathering had indeed heard of him as their expressions revealed. The subdued hostility that Lord Grantchester had shown to his presumptuous entrance seemed to give way to curiosity.

"You're the feller that's been involved in all these murders," he said.

Simon nodded.

"That's what I want to talk to you about."

"Me?" said his lordship in surprise.

"You," confirmed the Saint.

He looked at the puzzled faces of the others and saw no sense in alarming them.

"Just a brief private talk," he amplified.

Lord Grantchester considered the request for a moment and then shrugged.

"Very well, but it will have to be brief. We hold a fancy-dress ball every Christmas Eve and there's still a lot to be done."

As he crossed the room towards the Saint he glanced out at the snow.

"If they can all get here," he added, more to himself than his visitor. "Damn phone's out of order. Don't know who's coming and who ain't. Little bit of snow and the whole country grinds to a halt."

He led the way into the library and shut the door. They sat on either side of a fireless grate. The Saint explained his theory about the murders and then came to the reason for his visit.

"Were you the fourth person involved in Sir Basil's plans for the new faculty?"

Lord Grantchester nodded.

"Sir Basil knew I was a former student at St. Enoch's. He was quite honest about it. Said that a lord would attract the people whose money he was after." Lord Grantchester chuckled to himself. "I'm a director on the board of half a dozen companies and I'm not even sure what they do. People like to have a title on their letterheads."

He became serious again.

"This was a bit different, though. You see, there's a family trust. It was set up some years ago so that the blasted tax man wouldn't get everything when the head of the family snuffed it. The family draws salaries from the trust just as if it was a company. There's also a provision for donations to charities. Certain tax advantages, you understand. The idea was that St. Enoch's would put up thirty per cent of the money from its own resources. Sir Basil told me he was tapping three businessmen for twenty per cent each, and the Grantchester Trust would contribute the final ten per cent."

"But Sir Basil didn't say who those businessmen were?"

"I left it to him to find 'em. If their credit references were okay, they were okay with me. This was all way back in the autumn. I've been abroad since then. Can't stand the cold these days. Only come back for Christmas. Sir Basil wrote to me a couple of weeks ago saying everything was arranged. Could we all meet on Christmas Eve to sign the papers. Seemed in a bit of a hurry but I said it sounded fine. Subject to the audit, of course."

The Saint pounced on the word.

"Audit? What audit?"

Lord Grantchester chuckled again.

"See you're not a businessman, young feller," he said. "This may be charity but it's also business. We're not talking about a few quid, you know. By the time it was finished the whole thing was going to cost getting on for half a million."

The Saint whistled softly. He hadn't realised that so much money was involved.

Lord Grantchester continued: "Of course there would have to be an audit of the college's books. They were putting up the biggest single slice. Otherwise everyone else could have put up their money and then found the college couldn't meet its obligations. Then what? Damn easy to give money away, damn hard to get it back, especially when it's been turned into bricks and mortar."

The last segment of the puzzle slotted neatly into place.

"I think you should know," said the Saint deliberately, "that these murders you've been hearing about just happen to have eliminated Sir Basil's backers. With one remaining exception, so far as I've been able to find out."

His lordship might have been regarded by many as a stuffed shirt, but there was no doubt that it was a stuffing of excellent quality. He eyed the Saint with a calmly speculative expression.

"So you think this maniac who's murdered the others will have a go at me too?" he said at length.

"I'm sure of it," Simon replied firmly. "I'd like your

permission to search the house, and to hang around for a while."

Lord Grantchester pondered the request.

"Damn inconvenient," he muttered. "The family are here already and the first guests will be arriving soon. Don't want to alarm people."

"I promise not to alarm people," Simon told him. "But I do think that it's necessary. This man isn't a maniac. He's a cold calculating killer, and a fancy-dress ball would give him a perfect opening."

Lord Grantchester recognised the strength of the Saint's argument. He stood up.

"Very well. But please be as discreet as you can." He stopped at the door. "I'll tell the staff you're a surveyor."

"A surveyor?" the Saint repeated rather blankly.

"That's right. From the insurance company. The west wing is practically falling down. Been locked up for years because it's unsafe. Got to do something about it."

Simon smiled and promised to pose as a surveyor. What a surveyor would be doing working so late on Christmas Eve might be a difficult question to answer if he was challenged, but with luck it wouldn't be asked.

So the west wing, the oldest part of the house, was unsafe. So it was probably the best place for a break-in. So nobody went there any more, so it was safe as a hiding place. So he would start in the west wing. He told Lord Grantchester his intention and was given directions.

As he traversed the house towards the west wing he tried to put himself in the murderer's place. Would he break in early, hide, and wait for the fancy-dress ball to start, and then mingle with the guests until he saw an opportunity to strike? Or would he arrive among other guests, in costume, and hope to sneak in unchallenged?

The Saint decided that, since the weather might drastically reduce the numbers present, he'd opt for the first choice. If necessary, he could still hide and get at his victim when the household had gone to sleep.

He entered the west wing by a door on the ground floor, the only one, Lord Grantchester had told him, that was not kept locked.

In the manner of houses of its period, the ground floor was served by one long corridor that ran between all the rooms until it reached the far end of the wing. In the centre it spread out into a square-shaped hall with a flight of wooden stairs leading straight up to a balustraded gallery.

What little furniture remained in the rooms was shrouded in dust sheets which in the half-light looked like slumbering ghosts. The air was heavy with the smell of mould and damp and rotting woodwork. The Saint refrained from announcing his presence by switching on the lights or using his torch and made do with the moonlight that was helped by being reflected from the snow outside.

He checked all the downstairs rooms and returned to the hall. He climbed to the landing at the top of the stairs and considered his next move. From the gallery ran two passages, one towards the centre of the house, the other to the opposite end. He flipped a mental coin and came down in favour of the latter.

Here the corridor ran between other rooms and was so dark that he had no alternative but to switch on his flashlight. It was the shape and size of a fountain pen, with the small beam further restricted by silver foil pasted over the lens. It emitted only a pencil-thin ray, but his night vision was as keen as any cat's and it was enough.

He moved slowly and cautiously along the passage, his

ears straining to pick up any sound that might betray the presence of another intruder. He checked the rooms as he passed them without finding anyone. Of course there was no certainty that the killer was yet on the premises. And then the creak of a floorboard made him freeze.

He waited for what seemed minutes but was in reality no more than a few seconds. The sound came again, louder this time. His ears guided his eyes to the far end of the corridor where it formed a T junction with a similar passage leading towards the rear of the house, and in the deep gloom down there a hooded figure moved.

11

Simon smiled blissfully as he watched the dim shape of a Santa Claus disappear around the corner. And then he followed. Making less sound than a scavenging mouse, he reached the junction in time to see the figure enter a room a few yards to his right.

He edged along the wall towards the door, passing another as he did so, keeping close to the wall where the boards were less likely to creak.

Standing outside the door which he had seen the Santa Claus use, he listened to try and pinpoint whereabouts in the room the man was. By the time he heard the sound behind him it was already too late.

He felt the cold bluntness of a gun barrel against his neck.

"Inside," said a voice in his ear.

The Saint opened the door and stepped into the room. He had been caught bending in the past but he would have been prepared to admit that he had never been quite as doubled up as then.

He glanced around the room and saw that it had two doors, the one he had just come through and another a few feet away which he had ignored in his haste to reach the door the Santa had used. It made the most beautifully simple setup for an ambush, and he was sportsman enough to acknowledge it.

"Very, very clever," he said as he turned slowly to face his captor, being careful to make no sudden movement that might precipitate a bullet.

The Santa Claus was standing beside the now closed door. He reached out and switched on the light. He wore a full Santa Claus mask, from bushy white eyebrows to ruddy cheeks to white moustache and beard, but the Saint was not deceived.

"Merry Christmas, Godfrey," he said.

Nyall's eyes blinked through the holes in his mask. In his hand was a .38 revolver and it was levelled unwaveringly at the Saint's abdomen.

Simon looked at the gun with polite interest.

"A war souvenir?" he enquired pleasantly.

"That's right," said Nyall in an equally matter-of-fact tone. "Not as accurate as Denzil's match pistol, but good enough at this distance."

"I don't doubt it," Simon said.

The two men considered each other warily. The Saint had no illusions about the danger he faced, but the smile never left his lips even if it had left his eyes. Godfrey Nyall was the tenser of the two. He would obviously have to kill the Saint but his curiosity needed to be satisfied.

"You must be as clever as they say you are," he said. "How did you guess it was me?"

"I am even cleverer than they say I am," Simon replied. "I had my suspicions when I remembered that photo in your office and thought about how Casden had been killed. Then I thought it strange that the police should find the pistol in Rosco's room. It wasn't there when I looked, but of course you were going to replace it when I bumped into you in the corridor."

He paused. Nyall said nothing but continued to blink steadily at him. The Saint went on:

"I still couldn't find a motive. But there was Darslow's crack about economists. And that made me think back to those papers on your desk and the stories that had been ringed. Gilts and blue chip shares, you'd said. But those stories would have affected commodities, and they're too risky for a college to speculate in. Doing some dabbling on your own? Then his lordship mentioned an upcoming audit, and suddenly I saw the light."

Nyall continued to stare without speaking at the Saint, who, conscious that his one hope lay in playing for time, said: "Commodities are dangerous things. Buy or sell at a fixed price now for payment and delivery in a few months. If the price goes the way you're betting, you make a packet. But if it doesn't . . ."

"I was unlucky," Nyall broke in.

"So you borrowed from the college funds to make up the difference," said the Saint. "Easy enough for someone in your position. Until you heard about Sir Basil's plans and the audit."

"I had no alternative," said Nyall defensively. "It would have meant ruin, prison. There was only one way out."

"Good scheme, dressing as Father Christmas to kill

them all," Simon said. "But then I showed up and it began to go wrong."

"Why didn't you say anything before?" the bursar wanted to know.

"Because I needed some kind of proof, more than just the sort of clever theory that wraps up a storybook whodunit. The best way seemed to be to catch you red-handed on your next job. Which is what I've done."

"And much good it'll do you," Nyall said, now very coldly.

The Saint watched him deliberately raise the revolver to heart level.

"That thing makes quite a noise when it goes off," he ventured to remark.

"Nothing that's likely to be heard from this part of the house, through these walls," Nyall said.

Simon Templar stared death in the face and seemed to find it amusing. He brought his left hand up unhurriedly, his right hand pushing back his left cuff as if to give him a sight of his wrist watch. At the same time the fingers of his right hand slid into the sleeve to find the chased ivory hilt of the knife sheathed against his left forearm.

"I wonder if that fortuneteller was right about the exact time I'd get it," he murmured.

Nyall's knuckle whitened on the trigger, and in that split instant the Saint dived aside. His knife flashed through the air in the same second as the pistol cracked.

He felt the bullet pass his ear as he went down. He hit the deck and rolled over, conscious only that he was still alive, that the gamble had paid off.

He heard Nyall curse and the gun thud to the floor. As he rolled over he could see why. The razor-sharp blade had slashed the tendons at the base of the bursar's fingers. Which was not bad throwing, Simon told himself.

Nyall stared for a second at the blood that was dripping from his hand. And then he went after the gun. But that breathing spell had been all that the Saint needed. He flung himself across the floor and his fingertips touched the butt of the revolver first. Nyall, realising he could never pick it up before the Saint, did the only thing he could. He kicked out wildly. His toe caught the trigger guard, and the gun spun through the air to fall in the far corner of the room.

The Saint twisted around and his other hand cupped behind Nyall's ankle and pulled. Nyall tottered for a moment, his arms flailing as he tried to keep his balance, before he fell backwards. Simon maintained his grip and began to rise, but Nyall lashed out with his other foot and the heel of his shoe caught the Saint on the side of the head.

The stark lighting of the room was suddenly enhanced by a shower of tumbling golden stars. But the Saint was the only one who saw them. Involuntarily his hold weakened, and Nyall tore his other ankle free.

With a reflex action the Saint threw himself in the direction of the revolver, trying desperately to clear his head and brush away the sparks that still danced before his eyes as he prepared to meet a follow-up attack. But the attack never came.

Perhaps Nyall panicked. Perhaps his spirit was broken by having one hand made useless. Perhaps he remembered what he had heard about the Saint and realised he would ultimately have no chance against him anyway in single unarmed combat. Perhaps it was a combination of all three. All he positively knew was that Nyall hesitated and then turned and fled.

Simon pulled himself upright, the action dispelling the worst of the kick's aftereffects. Nyall had been unlucky. It had been a powerful blow but a glancing one. A few degrees different and the Saint might not have known what happened next.

He quickly gathered up the revolver and his knife before going out into the corridor.

Nyall had reached the far end. He turned, a grotesque silhouette in his costume against the light from a high arched window that ran from the floor almost to the ceiling at the end of the passage, and looked from the gun to the grim-set face of the man who held it.

"There's no way out, Godfrey," said the Saint softly.

Nyall shook his head slowly, making his false beard wag in an outlandish parody of the character whose disguise he had adopted.

"There's always a way out," he pronounced calmly and distinctly.

And before anyone could have stopped him, he turned and hurled himself at the glass.

Simon ran to the window and looked down. The redcoated figure of Santa Claus, sometime bursar of St. Enoch's College, Cambridge, lay spread-eagled in the thin carpet of snow beside the house like a broken toy.

"You silly twit," said the Saint. "You should have used the chimney."

12

It might have been a scene straight out of a Hollywood production of *A Christmas Carol.* A bright, cloudless sky shivered to the ringing of a thousand bells from a hundred towers and spires. A glistening white shroud of freshly fallen snow lay across rooftops and streets. Along the pavements, overcoated and muffled in scarves, people trudged home from church.

The picture-postcard perfection of his surroundings failed to move Simon Templar as he steered the Hirondel slowly through Cambridge. After the events of the past week he felt a strong desire to leave both Cambridge and Christmas far behind. His imagination drifted towards a palm-fringed beach and a warm sea, and he found the prospect of overstuffed turkey and stodgy plum pudding distinctly unappealing. But when Chantek had offered to cook him a Christmas dinner, saying that otherwise she would have to spend the day all alone, he had not had the heart to refuse in the face of her almost childish eagerness.

His tiredness contributed to his mood. It had been another long night.

Godfrey Nyall had died before the ambulance arrived, without regaining consciousness. Had it been an attempt to escape, a last desperate gamble, or suicide? The Saint would never know. And Superintendent Nutkin would be content to let a coroner's jury decide the answer.

Lord Grantchester's title and personality had awed the police into doing what they had to do so discreetly and unobtrusively that his guests would be quite unaware of what had happened until they read about it in their morning papers. He had insisted that the Saint must stay for the party, kitted out as an Arab in robes easily improvised from a couple of bed sheets, and welcome to shelter behind any alias he chose.

"Damn decent of you to take all that trouble to save my life, as if it had more than just a few more years to go anyway."

It would be untrue to say that the Saint had not enjoyed his privileged anonymity, but he had slipped away before midnight when it had been announced that all true identities must be disclosed.

Now as he eased the Hirondel into a parking space at his destination and cut the engine, he wondered if this afternoon dinner *à deux* would be an anticlimax or perhaps only a relaxing but banal denouement.

He was wrong in both guesses.

Chantek answered his knock, and his pessimism began to be undermined by her artless delight at seeing him. She was wearing a sarong patterned with pink and blue flowers, and a pearl necklace glowed against the gold of her skin.

"*Slamat datang,*" she said.

"*Slamat, chantek,*" he said, using her name as the compliment that she deserved.

There was nothing Dickensian about her perfume, which harmonised perfectly with the exotic cooking smells that came to his nostrils.

She ushered him into a large living room where the white walls were hung with brightly coloured paintings. On the table in small bowls and platters was set out a fascinating variety of mysterious preparations.

He turned to her and smiled.

"This is Christmas dinner?" he said.

Chantek returned his smile.

"That's right," she replied. "*My* kind of Christmas dinner. I hope you like *rijsttafel.*"

Her costume and the spicy aroma of the feast she had prepared matched his recent thoughts of warmer, lazier climes so perfectly that for a moment he was speechless. She looked at him anxiously, worried that he might be disappointed by the surprise.

The Saint's smile broadened. He picked up a glass of wine from the table and raised it in a toast.

"Darling," he said, "it's the crowning touch to one Christmas I'll never forget. Someday they'll write a song about it. I can almost hear it—'Some En-Chantekd Evening . . .'"

WATCH FOR THE SIGN
OF THE SAINT

HE WILL BE BACK